The man appeared capable of most any feat

The ledge protruded a mere four feet. The fact that they'd landed on it in the dark was a miracle and then Dani decided it wasn't a miracle at all. John had heard the approach of danger before the men even entered the house. He'd led her through the woods last night at breakneck speed without hitting the first obstacle. The light from the moon and the scarce stars had been meager at best.

His auditory and visual senses were clearly far above normal. His ability to heal... Just then Dani's gaze settled on his mouth. The lip that had been split last evening in the fight had mended to the point of hardly being visible at all. The jaw that should have been bruised and swollen showed no hint of having been damaged. *Incredible* was the first word that came to mind.

"Nothing will hurt you," John stated with a kind of knowing that unsettled her. "No one will get past me."

There was no doubt that she was in grave danger, but somehow she was safe with this mysterious stranger....

Dear Harlequin Intrigue Reader,

This month you'll want to have all six of our books to keep you company as you brave those April showers!

- Debra Webb kicks off THE ENFORCERS, her exciting new trilogy, with *John Doe on Her Doorstep*. And for all of you who have been waiting with bated breath for the newest installment in Kelsey Roberts's THE LANDRY BROTHERS series, we have *Chasing Secrets*.

- Rebecca York, Ann Voss Peterson and Patricia Rosemoor join together in *Desert Sons*. You won't want to miss this unique three-in-one collection!

- Two of your favorite promotions are back. You won't be able to resist Leona Karr's ECLIPSE title, *Shadows on the Lake*. And you'll be on the edge of your seat while reading Jean Barrett's *Paternity Unknown*, the latest installment in TOP SECRET BABIES.

- Meet another of THE PRECINCT's rugged lawmen in Julie Miller's *Police Business*.

Every month you can depend on Harlequin Intrigue to deliver an array of thrilling romantic suspense and mystery. Be sure you read each one!

Sincerely,

Denise O'Sullivan
Senior Editor
Harlequin Intrigue

DEBRA WEBB

John Doe on Her Doorstep

HARLEQUIN®

TORONTO • NEW YORK • LONDON
AMSTERDAM • PARIS • SYDNEY • HAMBURG
STOCKHOLM • ATHENS • TOKYO • MILAN • MADRID
PRAGUE • WARSAW • BUDAPEST • AUCKLAND

I think we all go through a time in our lives
when we don't really know who we are or what we want to do.
Well, lucky for me, I met someone who made an incredible
difference in my life at a truly crucial juncture. She read my
first completed manuscript and proudly proclaimed it
"Romance!" That day was the beginning of a very exciting
journey for me. This book is dedicated to Patty Godfrey,
a dear friend and lovely Christian. Thank you, Patty,
for pointing me in the right direction.

ISBN 0-373-22837-6

JOHN DOE ON HER DOORSTEP

Copyright © 2005 by Debra Webb

All rights reserved. Except for use in any review, the reproduction or
utilization of this work in whole or in part in any form by any electronic,
mechanical or other means, now known or hereafter invented, including
xerography, photocopying and recording, or in any information storage
or retrieval system, is forbidden without the written permission of the
publisher, Harlequin Enterprises Limited, 225 Duncan Mill Road,
Don Mills, Ontario, Canada M3B 3K9.

All characters in this book have no existence outside the imagination of
the author and have no relation whatsoever to anyone bearing the same
name or names. They are not even distantly inspired by any individual
known or unknown to the author, and all incidents are pure invention.

This edition published by arrangement with Harlequin Books S.A.

® and TM are trademarks of the publisher. Trademarks indicated with
® are registered in the United States Patent and Trademark Office, the
Canadian Trade Marks Office and in other countries.

www.eHarlequin.com

Printed in U.S.A.

ABOUT THE AUTHOR

Debra Webb was born in Scottsboro, Alabama, to parents who taught her that anything is possible if you want it badly enough. When her husband joined the military, they moved to Berlin, Germany, and Debra became a secretary in the commanding general's office. By 1985 they were back in the States, and with the support of her husband and two beautiful daughters, Debra took up writing full-time and in 1998 her dream of writing for Harlequin came true. You can write to Debra with your comments at P.O. Box 64, Huntland, Tennessee 37345 or visit her Web site at www.debrawebb.com to find out exciting news about her next book.

Books by Debra Webb

CAST OF CHARACTERS

Adam (John Doe)—An Enforcer whose mission it is to eliminate the three known targets who betrayed the creator of the "super" gene, Dr. Daniel Archer, and to recover the file containing the key to the "super" gene formula.

Dani Archer—Could she really be responsible for her own father's murder?

Dr. Daniel Archer—The scientist who held the key to the "super" gene code.

Doc—A close family friend. The only real family Dani has left.

Rand and Cal—Two young men who help Dani out on the ranch and who may be responsible for bringing trouble to her door.

Sheriff Lane Nichols—One man Dani tries hard to stay clear of.

Director Richard O'Riley—Center director. He has the power to end lives. Has he made a mistake setting this mission into motion?

Congressman Terrence Winslow—The head of the Collective leaves the day-to-day operations to O'Riley. No one can connect him to trouble at Center.

Joseph Marsh—A project manager at Center. Is he friend or foe?

UN Secretary Donald Thurlo—He overstepped his bounds...got greedy.

Investigator Scott Davidson—Did Dani make a mistake going to him?

Cain—The most deadly Enforcer at Center. Most call him heartless. Director O'Riley calls him the best.

Prologue

Alexandria, Virginia
Weekend home of UN Secretary-General
Donald Thurlo

"Dammit."

Donald Thurlo shuffled through the mound of papers on his desk again. A pool of golden light from the brass lamp spilled over the mass of now insignificant correspondence scattered on the mahogany surface. Where the hell was that letter? He needed the damned letter. It was his only protection.

He'd taken it from his wall safe only a few minutes ago. His brow furrowed in concentration. What had he done after that? He'd rushed upstairs to throw a few things into a bag. He glanced at the Louis Vuitton case waiting at his feet. His pulse quickened. He had to get the hell out of here.

But first he had to have that damned letter.

"Looking for this?"

Ice-cold fear surged anew through Thurlo's veins. Slowly, he looked up from his desk.

Oh, God.

Too late.

With a pistol in his right hand, the stranger reached into the pocket of his leather jacket with his left and produced a folded piece of paper.

The letter.

Dammit.

Thurlo straightened and stared into the startling blue eyes of the assassin who'd been sent to silence him. "Why does it have to be *this* way?" he asked, his words trembling, fear coursing through him. "I could—"

"There's nothing you can do now," the man said in a deep, steady voice that proved more unnerving than if he'd screamed his response. "Goodbye, Mr. Secretary."

Thurlo started to cry for mercy, but the bullet's impact stunned him into silence....

Chapter One

Eastern Virginia

The early morning weather was perfect. The sun was shining now, spilling its glow over the evergreen landscape, the air clean and brisk from the October morning's frost. Not a cloud in the sky.

A perfect day for vengeance.

The first phase of his mission had been completed.

Adam slowed and took the next exit off I-95 South. His destination was centrally located between Alexandria and Richmond. Ten miles west of a small town called Hickory Grove, in Virginia's Caroline County.

Estimated time of arrival, he glanced at his watch, 1200 hours. Interrogation wouldn't take more than thirty minutes, termination about two seconds.

Then it would be finished.

His lips compressed into a grim line. Part of him would just as soon someone else from Center had been selected for this particular assignment. He was trained to put all emotion aside when it came to his work. Emotion had no place in this business. Thus, the paradox of today's mission. Director O'Riley had insisted that he was the best choice…the only choice despite the emotional connection. There was no question about that, Adam knew. No one at Center was better than he was. It wasn't ego; it was a simple fact.

So, for the first time since his activation eight years ago, Adam's mission was personal. Under normal circumstances Center ensured that an Enforcer's targets were unknown to him on a personal level. But not this time. He was more than simply familiar with the target's profile.

Adam summoned the image of his target. She wasn't the kind of woman a man could easily forget…even if he wanted to. He'd dreamed of those dark eyes and lush lips too many times to count. That would never happen again. He gritted his teeth now at the mere thought of her. The dream had turned into a nightmare. A nightmare that should never have been allowed to escalate out of control.

Today it would end. Justice would be served and the Judas would be cut down.

A muscle flexed rhythmically in his tightly clenched jaw as he considered the man, an innocent, good man, who had lost his life because of this traitor. Adam still faulted O'Riley, Center's operations director, for not anticipating this threat. He should have had Archer protected, at least for a while after his retirement. O'Riley damn sure should have known that Archer was keeping a copy of his research files at his private residence. What kind of security was Center running these days?

Adam had just returned from a mission in South Africa. He regretted his two-week absence now. Never before had he experienced such intense remorse. Had he been here, perhaps he somehow could have prevented Archer's death, though he couldn't see how immediately. There had to have been a way. No matter. It was done.

But he was here now, and he would avenge the death of his mentor. One of those involved in the murder had been taken care of already, which left at least one other key player besides the Judas. The identity of that second key player had not been confirmed at this point. But the Judas, his next target, was someone he knew well. Fire rekindled in Adam's gut. She had levied the ultimate betrayal, had pretended to love Daniel Archer. There would be no swift execution for this target. A slow, painful death was in order. Adam knew precisely how to make that happen.

Center had narrowed down the possibilities of who was behind the move to obtain Archer's research. A secret coalition called the Concern was the most logical culprit. Intel about the group was sparse, their leader ambiguous. What little Center did know about the group was not good. The few members tagged thus far were connected to scumbag Third World leaders. Concern's base of operations was thought to be in South America, but Center had not pinpointed the exact location yet.

Bastards. Fury tightened Adam's throat. He intended to be on the team that brought down every single member of that ruthless group. But that undertaking had not been sanctioned by the Collective yet. For the time being, Adam would have to placate himself with his current mission—terminating the Judas who had betrayed Archer.

Daniel Archer had been more than his mentor, he had been Adam's friend. Archer was the scientist who'd taken the Eugenics Project from the brink of failure to unparalleled success. A great man who cared deeply for his work, whose compassion went beyond friend and family to mankind in general. How ironic that his betrayal had come at the hands of the one person whom Archer trusted the most, loved the most—his own daughter.

Undeniable proof that relying on one's emotions was a mistake. A mistake Adam had no intention of ever making himself. It wasn't likely that he or any of the other Enforcers would ever find themselves in that kind of up close and personal relationship. Still, they were only human. He laughed, the sound strangely loud after the hours of silence. Despite their superior genetic coding, he supposed it wouldn't be impossible to fall into an emotional trap.

He never allowed his emotions to show, not even remotely. It wasn't that he lacked a full range, to some degree; it was simply that he maintained a strict control over himself. Discipline was the key. That was just one of the reasons he was so good at his work.

He smiled, thinking of what his friend Cain would say about who was the best Enforcer at Center. Adam knew there were those who would like to argue, but the proof was a matter of Center record. Number of failed missions: zero. His skills were unmatched, his instincts always on the money. He was the man for this job.

O'Riley wasn't taking chances with this mission. He wanted it done right the first time, and Adam would see to it that it was done with the cold, exacting precision of a surgeon's scalpel.

He forced away the memories of how Daniel Archer had doted on his supposedly loving daughter. Those heartfelt stories had worked their way under Adam's skin. Made him feel as if he knew the woman himself. And he did, on the outside. He would know her anywhere he saw her. Knew the music she loved, the movies she watched, even her favorite foods. But he hadn't known the evil that had lurked inside her. Even her father hadn't known that.

Tension radiating inside him, making him restless, Adam glanced at his watch once more. It would be over soon, he reminded himself. He took a deep breath and forced himself to relax. He would put this chapter of his life and all its memories behind him after today…but he would never forget. He would keep the coming moment tightly compartmentalized, only to be opened when he needed a reminder of what love and trust could do to a man. Of how emotions could betray even the strongest or most innocent of the species.

A car parked on the side of the road a mile or so in the distance dragged his attention from his less-than-pleasant thoughts. The hood was raised. Engine trouble. Adam slowed only slightly and surveyed the situation as he approached the vehicle. There were no houses on this section of the two-lane road. Traffic was sparse. In fact, since leaving the interstate he hadn't met the first vehicle. There might not be another one coming along for several hours.

A woman, twenty, twenty-five maybe, stepped slightly away from the front of the car as he slowly passed it. She held a small child in her arms.

A scowl tugged at Adam's brow as he pulled over to the side of the road in front of the woman's car. He scanned the area once more in his usual cautious manner as he emerged from his rental car and adjusted the Glock at the small of his back. He closed the door, taking another quick look at his watch. He didn't like delays, but he couldn't leave the woman and child stranded on the side of the road. He doubted even Cain would be that heartless. Adam smiled to himself. Well, maybe Cain would have driven on without stopping.

But not Adam. The least he could do was allow her to call a friend or family member for help on his cellular telephone. Five minutes, tops, and he'd be back on his way.

The woman shaded her eyes from the sun with her free hand and peered up at him as he approached. The child studied him curiously, a half-empty bottle clutched in his hand. Or maybe it was a girl. Adam hadn't spent any time around kids. Babies all looked alike to him.

"I don't know what happened," the woman explained. "It just died on me," she added, gesturing to the engine. "I barely got it off the road. I'm sure glad you came along. I was afraid I'd be waiting half the day."

Adam sensed her uneasiness. He was a tall, broad-shouldered man. This was a deserted stretch of road. She had a right to be uneasy. But at the moment, in her eyes, he supposed he was the lesser of the two evils, even if he did make her a little nervous.

He didn't look directly at her as he stepped between her and the car. No point in making her any more jumpy than she already was. He took a look at the exposed engine as he reached into his jacket pocket and fished out his cell phone.

"Why don't you call a friend?" he suggested. He offered the phone in an effort to set her at ease as he surveyed the engine. Something wasn't right.

"Thank you." Her voice still sounded a little uncertain, but she took the telephone from him.

His gaze narrowed as his senses assimilated a number of inconsistencies. No heat rising, no ticking sound of the engine cooling.

The engine was cold.

"Have you been waiting long?" He cut a look in her direction as he waited for a response.

She shook her head, her eyes carefully averted from his. "Five minutes, maybe less."

She was lying.

"I'm just glad you came along," she repeated, her voice too cheery as she pressed a series of numbers on the keypad, then lifted the phone to her ear.

Not enough digits. Any local call in this part of the state would be a long distance one on his phone, requiring one and the area code. When she made no move to redial his suspicion was confirmed.

The sound of frosted grass crushing beneath a heavy footstep came from his left.

Adam started to reach for his weapon.

"Don't move, man!" a male voice commanded.

Young, nervous.

Adam felt the unmistakable cold, hard barrel of a pistol press between his shoulder blades.

"You don't want to do this," Adam told him quietly. There was no way to disguise the element of danger in his tone. It was instinctive. The shakily exhaled breath behind him told him the guy had noticed it as well.

"What're you doing?" the woman asked, her voice rising with hysteria as she flung the cell phone to the ground. "You didn't say nothing about guns, Jimmy!" The child in her arms whimpered as if he sensed her anxiety.

"Shut up," the guy, Jimmy, growled. "You said my name, you stupid bitch!"

"Put the gun away, Jimmy, and we'll forget this ever happened," Adam suggested. He didn't have time for this crap. He thought highwaymen had gone out of style about a hundred years ago. The last thing he needed was a nervous one. If he could distract the guy, he might have the opportunity to go for his own weapon.

The scrape of a boot heel in the gravel on the side of the road sounded a few feet away.

Adam stilled, listening. Jimmy hadn't moved. Neither had the woman. Someone else had joined their little party.

The distinct scent of cheap aftershave hit Adam's nostrils.

Another man. Jimmy wasn't wearing any deodorant, much less any aftershave. Adam could smell his sweat. Jimmy was scared...the other guy presented an unknown variable with his silence. Adam knew instinctively that the unknown enemy was a far more serious threat. His tension escalated to a new level.

"What's he doing here?" the woman protested. Her child's perpetual fretting underscored her mounting fear.

"Say good night, big guy."

Not Jimmy's voice. The other man's.

Adam reached for his weapon. His fingers curled around the pistol grip at the same instant that he prepared to pivot toward the threat.

Something crashed into his skull before he could turn. White flashes speared through his brain. His knees buckled. Another blow. He jerked with the impact of it. Brilliant points of light stabbed behind his clenched lids. He had to…

But it was already too late.

Ghost Mountain, Colorado
Center

RICHARD O'RILEY scanned the latest report on the Judas mission. One target had been eliminated, but not the second. He looked up at the man seated on the other side of his cluttered desk. "Still no word on our man?"

Dupree, Center's top analyst, shook his head. "Nothing. Either his TD has malfunctioned or he's dead."

O'Riley's jaw clenched. Adam was the best Enforcer they had. And O'Riley wasn't ready to give up on him yet. Electronic devices malfunctioned from time to time. It wasn't impossible, just not probable. With the tracking devices neurologically implanted, they stopped functioning only when the host stopped breathing. Unless, of course, there was a malfunction, which had to be the case now. O'Riley refused to believe anything else at this point.

"He's only been out of the loop for twenty-four hours," O'Riley pointed out. "No matter how it looks, we're going to keep an open mind. I know Adam. Whatever has gone down on this mission, I can assure you he's been in tighter spots. He'll figure a way out."

At least Dupree had the good sense to keep his mouth shut instead of arguing. O'Riley was well aware of how he felt. Dupree had weighed the known data, ran simulations and assessed all the variables, but O'Riley didn't give a damn. This was his operation. He would say when it was time to give up on Adam, and that wouldn't be anytime soon. A team had already been dispatched to retrace Adam's steps.

Dupree stood, clearly frustrated but lacking the necessary nerve to push the issue. "We'll keep monitoring local law enforcement activities. We know Adam left Alexandria. Considering the time that his TD went down, I'd say he was about halfway to the primary target, maybe closer. If he's been in an accident of some sort, we'll hear about it soon enough. There can't be that much going on along that sleepy stretch of country road. The recon team will be reporting in any time now. They hit ground zero about twenty minutes ago."

When Dupree had left his office, O'Riley tossed the status report aside. Dupree was an uptight ass, but the best intel analyst on staff at Center. O'Riley released a heavy breath. This whole situation stunk. First, Daniel Archer is murdered; then, Donald Thurlo's betrayal is discovered and Joseph Marsh is suddenly missing; now this. He didn't like it. He didn't like it at all. He couldn't shake the feeling that something vital was missing from the scenario. Something he and all these highly trained, overpaid intel analysts were missing.

The Eugenics Project was far too valuable to risk for any reason. Anyone involved in this mess would be eliminated. Too tired to think as clearly as he should, O'Riley rubbed his eyes with his thumb and forefinger.

He stood and turned to stare out the window of his office. The scene beyond the specially designed outer shell that encased the entire building was slightly distorted, but welcome nonetheless. Sometimes he hated the copper-lined walls and soundproof glass of this place. Hated it, but it was, undeniably, necessary.

Though Center was located on a remote mountain in Colorado, it was still vulnerable. Ghost Mountain was owned by the U.S. government, operated by the Collective and heavily guarded with state-of-the-art security systems. No one outside this building knew the identities of those who worked inside. But even with those extreme measures in place, secrets could still escape.

They'd just learned that the hard way.

A technology war had long since replaced the Cold War. They weren't fighting the KGB moles and double agents anymore. Now it was the *code* war and some computer geek sitting in a dark room listening to their every uttered word and computer keystroke. The weapons of today were every imaginable kind of electronic and laser device for stealing bytes of communication via the Net, fax or any one of numerous other analog or digital means of transmission. Nothing was sacred anymore.

Of course, all secrets weren't necessarily stolen. Some violations of security were merely mistakes.

Fatal mistakes.

Archer had known better. The risk he'd taken by keeping a copy of his files, encrypted or not, at home was a very dumb move for such an intelligent man. In the end, he'd had to pay the ultimate price for that error in judgment.

If Adam failed, which was a highly unlikely scenario assuming he was still alive, they would send another man to finish the job.

Adam had never failed before. O'Riley wasn't ready to admit that he had this time.

He turned back to his desk and looked at the open dossier lying there. Adam. Thirty years old. Six foot two, one hundred and eighty pounds. The cream of the crop. IQ: immeasurable. Physical condition: perfect. Skill level: unmatched. No one in the program was quite as good.

Well, O'Riley confessed, there was one who could hold his own with Adam. *Cain.* But there was one key element that marred Cain's track record. He was every bit as skilled as Adam but lacked any capacity for compassion or any other essential emotion. That missing component limited his usefulness in many situations. Thankfully, Archer had observed that deficit and all who'd come after Cain, the original prototype, were better for it.

Archer. It was still hard for O'Riley to believe he was dead. They'd worked together for more than twenty years. How could something as simple as a thoughtless mistake lead to this? He shook his head, weary of trying to make sense of it all. It was done. There was no way to change it. O'Riley could only see that the traitors were eliminated. The identity of the primary Judas made the situation unbelievable.

He refused to analyze it any further. It had to be done, regardless of his reservations or his personal feelings. No one regretted the decision any more than he did. Joseph Marsh would be next, if they could find him. Fury twisted in O'Riley's chest. He would like to kill that son of a bitch with his own hands. He had to be guilty…otherwise, he wouldn't have vanished into thin air. Well, Marsh could run, but he couldn't hide forever. They would find him and when they did, he would die.

For the moment, O'Riley would be happy if Adam just reported in and let him know what was going on.

There had to be a reasonable explanation for why his tracking device had failed. O'Riley was unwilling to accept that he was dead.

Not yet, anyway.

Chapter Two

Virginia
Archer Ranch

At the sound of a sputtering engine, Dani Archer paused in her trek from the barn to the house. She lifted her hand to shield her eyes from the early morning sun and smiled as she watched the rickety old blue truck bounce down the mountain road on the back of her property. Hunting season was still a couple of weeks away and already the boys were scouting out the best locations in which to set up their tree stands. She inhaled long and deep, relishing the underlying scent of the lush evergreens cloaking the eastern Virginia landscape.

Her smile faded as she considered that if her father hadn't allowed those two to hunt on this land since they were barely big enough to handle rifles, she wouldn't now. Especially after hearing those gunshots yesterday morning.

Hunting was totally barbaric. To her way of thinking, anything one wanted to eat should be purchased at the local market, not hunted down and shot. Tucking her fingers into the pockets of her jeans, she walked out to the edge of the dirt road and waited for the truck to reach her.

She supposed that, basically, it was the same thing. Someone had killed the animals that ended up as hamburger or pork chops, but buying the products at the market seemed so much more civilized than bringing a carcass home strapped across the hood of one's vehicle.

The truck skidded to a stop in front of her and a smile lifted her lips once more. She could handle a few minutes of company this morning. And she needed to ask about those gunshots she'd heard. "Hello, boys."

"Howdy, Miss Dani," Calvin Peacock offered first. "You're looking mighty pretty today." That wicked grin he'd perfected to an art form slid across his face. At nineteen, he was more than a little full of himself.

Randall Williams, the driver, bopped Calvin on the head with his camouflaged cap. "Stop flirting, Cal. Miss Dani ain't interested in nothing you've got."

Cal glared at his friend who was a year younger. "Shut up, Rand. Don't make me have to kick your butt," he warned.

Rand huffed in disbelief. "Like you could."

"Now, now, gentlemen," Dani cut in as she propped her arms in the open passenger-side window and studied the two young men. "You know I love you both, but I can't tolerate your incessant pissing contest."

Rand blushed. Cal looked a bit sheepish himself.

"You guys preparing for hunting season already?" she inquired, knowing the answer before she asked.

"'Course," Cal said. "I mean, that's the way we've always done it. Mr. Archer didn't mind. That's okay with you, isn't it?"

"Sure. Just be careful." She considered their camouflage attire. "Aren't you supposed to wear something orange to make yourselves visible to other hunters?" No one else had permission to be hunting on the land. It was posted, but some people ignored the signs.

"No way," Rand enthused. "We like to blend in. There ain't supposed to be nobody else up there anyway."

"That brings me to my next question," she ventured, almost dreading the answer. "I thought I heard a couple of shots fired around this time yesterday morning. You guys don't know anything about that, do you?" She looked from one to the other. "I mean, the season hasn't even opened yet," she added, hoping neither of them had been doing anything he shouldn't have.

Rand's gaze bumped into Cal's and he looked away quickly…too quickly.

Dani frowned at the covert move. "What?" She directed the question at Cal since he was the oldest.

"He thinks—"

"Shut up, Cal," Rand snapped.

Worry tightened Dani's chest. "Look, fellas, my father has allowed the two of you to hunt on that mountain since you were kids. And I don't mind that the tradition continues. But if you're keeping anything from me, well…then I'll mind."

Rand dropped his chin to his chest and blew out a resigned breath, then turned to her, albeit reluctantly. "I don't know for sure that it was what I thought," he told her finally. "I didn't see…exactly. Just a glimpse."

"The knucklehead thinks he shot a man," Cal explained with a snort of disbelief. "I tried to tell him it was nothing but a deer or a bear, but his head's as thick as a block."

Fear trickled down her spine. "Shut the truck off, Rand," she ordered.

"Damnation," he complained, but did as he was told.

"Start at the beginning." Her tone left no room for protest from either of them.

"I thought it was a deer," Rand began without looking at her. "I got excited and fired. I know I shouldn't have."

"That sounds just as stupid now as it did then," Cal said. "I thought the world had come to an end the way you were squealing like a girl."

Rand glared at him for two long beats before shifting his attention back to Dani. "Anyway, when whatever it was darted deeper into the woods…" He hesitated, clearly not looking forward to telling her the rest. "I could've sworn it was a man."

"Get over it, Rand, it *was not* a man," Cal ground out. "You're getting Miss Dani upset for no reason."

Dani moistened her lips and swallowed at the sensation tightening the back of her throat. "And this happened yesterday?"

"Yeah," Rand admitted balefully.

"Did you see anything this morning?"

Cal shrugged. "We did find some blood, but, hell, there would've been blood whatever he hit, four-legged or two-legged."

Dani resisted the urge to shudder. There was no point in overreacting. Cal was probably right. "But you didn't find any tracks or...or a body?"

Rand shook his head. "No way. Nothing but the blood."

"Nothing," Cal confirmed. "And we looked around real good."

"You're not going to call the sheriff, are you?" Rand looked scared and suddenly far younger than his years.

The sheriff. Yeah, right. She wouldn't call the sheriff if—

Don't go there, Dani, she ordered silently, the mere thought of the man's voice already making her sick to her stomach. She wouldn't go down that road again. The sheriff was a total jerk. He wasn't worth the brainpower it took to think of him.

"Well, we'll just have to assume that it was a deer or a bear. Cal seems to think so. I guess that's good enough for me." She straightened, confident in her decision.

Rand looked weak with relief.

"I want you guys to take extra care up there from now on. Just to be on the safe side. Deer season brings out the worst in people who want nothing more than another trophy to hang on their wall."

Both agreed and Dani waved goodbye as the truck lurched forward. She watched until they reached the main highway and turned toward town. The two were good guys, especially considering their ages. While most kids were out drinking and discovering just how much trouble they could get into, Rand and Cal preferred hunting and fishing. She'd been the same as a teenager, never one to go looking for trouble. She'd loved riding and spent what others considered their tumultuous years engrossed in horses and riding gear.

Mulling over their story, she headed in the direction of the house. Cal was older and more mature than Rand. If he wasn't worried, then she shouldn't be.

The screen door whined as she pulled it open and stepped into the bright, airy kitchen. Her stomach rumbled as she inhaled the scent of freshly baked blueberry muffins. She'd left them on the counter to cool this morning before going out to feed the horses.

Coffee and a warm, homemade muffin would be good about now. And maybe the food would soothe her frayed nerves. She shivered again at the notion that the blood might not have come from an animal. Surely if it had been a man, he'd have called out to the boys. Or, at the very least, have come down for help. She flinched when she recalled the echoing sound of the shots she'd heard.

Pushing those unsettling thoughts aside, she reached for the coffeepot. She had work to do. Work she'd already put off for too long.

The telephone rang.

Startled by the unexpected sound, Dani stared at the beige instrument as it rang two more times. Doc was out of town today, so she doubted it was him. She glanced at the clock—eight o'clock. Since the few friends she had were on Pacific time she felt certain it wasn't any of them calling so early. A sales call, maybe? The fourth ring prompted her into action and she picked up the receiver.

"Hello."

"Dr. Archer, this is Dr. Feldon."

The hospital administrator. Though it was five in San Diego, that particular point was obviously no deterrent to her boss. Dani resisted the urge to groan. She wasn't ready to talk to him just yet.

"Good morning, Dr. Feldon," she returned, though considering the tale she'd heard from Rand and this phone call, there was nothing good about it.

"I hate to disturb you," he said quietly, but Dani could hear the underlying tension in his voice. "I know this has been a difficult time, but I was hoping you'd reached some sort of decision by now as to when you plan to return to work."

Dani stretched the phone cord and dropped into a chair at the kitchen table. She squeezed her eyes shut. Dr. Feldon wanted her final decision. And since he hadn't called even once during the past two weeks, chances were he was through waiting patiently.

"I completely sympathize with your loss," he went on, distress joining the tension in his tone, "and I don't want to have to rush you, but the board is on my case. Your leave of absence runs out next week and I need to know if you're coming back."

A heavy silence settled between them. Dani could picture him sitting behind his desk, the phone clutched to his ear and the fingers of his free hand doing an annoying little drumming routine on his blotter pad. She knew he hadn't looked forward to making this call any more than she'd looked forward to receiving it, but he had every right to know her plans.

"I'm sorry I haven't called you already, Dr. Feldon," she told him sincerely. She should have. "But to be honest with you, I've been putting it off."

"Look, Dani," he said, dropping formality. "I know your father was the only family you had and that the two of you were very close, but life does go on. You must know that you can't hide from it forever." He sighed. "From what you've told me about your father, he wouldn't want you to. I went out on a limb by granting this extended leave to a resident. You're an excellent doctor and I don't want to lose you. But I can't put this off any longer."

"I understand. I'll give you my decision no later than the end of this week. Thank you for your patience, Dr. Feldon." He had been good to her and she'd taken advantage by putting off the call he'd expected last week.

He agreed and they exchanged goodbyes. Dani moved back to the counter and hung the receiver in its cradle. A fresh wave of emptiness and loss washed over her, leaving behind a shoulder load of indecision.

She wanted to go back to her life. She really did…but she just couldn't seem to work up the initiative. She slumped into her chair and propped her chin in her hands. Her work fulfilled her professionally. She loved the hospital at which she'd been lucky enough to be invited to do her residency. But things were different now. Nothing felt right anymore. Once she was back on the west coast, how often would she manage to get back here? Her dad had been the incentive more than the place. He was gone now. What would become of her horses? Rand and Cal would gladly exercise them, but it wasn't the same.

She glanced at the muffins and coffee waiting for her. Her appetite had died. Just like everything else in her life. First, her mother, when she had been only ten years old, and now, her father. It just wasn't fair. As an only child, she had no one left. Her mother had been an only child as well. Both her grandparents on her mother's side had passed away before Dani was born. The few living relatives she had left were on her father's side, and he'd been estranged from his family since he'd married her mother more than thirty years ago. She barely knew their names.

The bottom line was, she was alone. She'd never felt that way before…not once. Though her father'd had a demanding position with the government, he'd always managed to be there for her. He'd seen that she was educated in the best private schools near his work so that they could be together as much as possible, and her nanny had proven more second mother than hired help. She'd died, too, shortly after Dani's graduation from medical school.

She looked around the big old country-style kitchen and exhaled a weary sound. This place was all she had left of the life she'd shared with her father. They'd spent every holiday and vacation here since she was twelve. He'd bought the mini horse ranch for the sole purpose of nudging her back into riding. Oh, he'd said that it would be his retirement home, and it had been, but Dani knew the real reason he'd bought the place. She'd given up riding after her mother's death. Horses had been Lorna Archer's passion. She'd ridden like the wind and Dani had loved riding with her. Riding had been their special time.

After her mother's accident, Dani had thought she might never ride again. But her father and this place had helped her put that hurt behind her. They'd both come to love the twenty acres nestled against the foothills of Virginia mountains and miles away from the nearest signs of civilization.

After his retirement just six months ago, her father had sold his Georgetown apartment and moved here permanently. The plan was he'd be here full time and she'd take every possible long weekend and all of her vacation time to be with him. To escape the hectic pace of city life. To get back into riding again. For her last birthday he'd bought her two new horses. The gelding she'd loved as a teenager had had to be put down last year. She'd been devastated and swore she would never own another. She didn't have time for riding anyway, she'd rationalized. But when her father had introduced her to the beautiful animals, she'd fallen in love instantly. Life was right again.

Then her father had died. She closed her eyes and tried to force away the horrible memories. A freak accident, they'd called it. He'd fallen off the barn where he'd been nailing down a piece of loose metal roofing and broken his neck. She couldn't imagine what had possessed him to attempt the work himself. In the past, he'd always called a local handyman. But not this time. And now she was alone. Who would help her put this hurt behind her?

There was no one.

"Enough, Archer," she scolded as she got to her feet. She had a decision to make. And chores to do.

That was the good thing about running a ranch on her own, even a small one. There was always plenty she had to do. Cal and Rand had offered time and again to give her a hand, but she preferred doing the work herself. It gave her a sense of purpose.

Not to mention that it occupied her mind.

She shut off the coffeepot and poured the steaming brew down the drain. The muffins she stored in the bread keeper in case she got hungry later. She rinsed the white porcelain sink and dried her hands. There was no point in rehashing what might have been. As much as she'd love to, she couldn't bring her father back.

Returning to her job in California was the right thing to do. It was what her father would want her to do. The training she would receive at such a renowned learning hospital was priceless. Then she could settle back here and take Doc's place when he retired, *if* she still wanted to when the time came. Her father and Doc, the small community's only physician, had plotted that career choice for her years ago. They'd teased her that no one else would ever be good enough to replace Doc but her.

She wasn't sure she could do that now. She wasn't sure of anything anymore.

Whatever she decided to do, a few years at Mercy General would be a tremendous boost to her skill level. Mercy was known far and wide for its cutting-edge technology and for pushing the envelope where research and patient care were concerned. Whether she was a small-town doctor or worked in a larger hospital, she wanted to be the best she could be.

Besides, this wasn't the kind of opportunity one walked away from. She recognized that fact, even if she hadn't wanted to think about leaving the home she and her father loved so much. He would want her to get on with her life. It was time.

"Past time," she told herself firmly.

She should just call Dr. Feldon back and tell him she would return to work a week from Monday. He would be relieved and so would she. No point in prolonging the inevitable. Ten days was plenty of time to finish her business here and close up the house. Cal and Rand would take care of the horses. All she had to do was firm up the deal. Doc, Cal and Rand would drop by and check on the place regularly. There was no reason for her to stay. No reason at all.

Except that she felt close to her father here. And his death just didn't sit right with her. No matter that two weeks had passed, she still felt disconnected… unsettled. Maybe that feeling would never go away as long as she was here. Maybe that was the whole problem. Dani paused in the entry hall and studied the collage of framed photographs lovingly placed on the table there. Tears welled in her eyes as her gaze moved from one precious memory to the other. She might never be whole again until she put all this behind her.

Putting off the inevitable even one more day would be irresponsible. Her father was gone and she missed him terribly. But, Dr. Feldon was right. Life does go on.

It was time for her to join the living again.

She could start by making that call.

THE TELEPHONE RANG. He didn't want to answer. He knew who it would be. But he had to. Otherwise he might just end up dead, too.

"Hello," he said trying hard to hide his fear.

"Tell me you've found it," the voice on the other end of the line snapped.

"I've looked everywhere. I can't—"

"I don't want to hear excuses! Didn't you read your paper yesterday? Thurlo is dead. How long do you think it'll be before they send someone for one of us?"

He scrubbed a shaky hand over his face. He'd read the paper all right. "I'm doing my best—"

"That isn't good enough." The accusation was a savage growl. "You find that file or we're both dead. You don't make deals like this and then drag your feet. They won't wait much longer."

They. If Center didn't kill him, *they* probably would.

"I'll find it." It was all he could think to say. It was what he had to do. He didn't need reminding.

"Call me the instant you find it."

"I will."

"And don't forget, I want all loose ends tied up. *She* is your problem. Do what you have to."

"I understand."

He hung up the phone and closed his eyes. Dear God, what had he done? His eyes opened and he squared his shoulders as reality seared through him. He'd done what he had to.

He swallowed back the vile taste of self-loathing.

And he'd do it again.

Whatever the cost.

Chapter Three

Ghost Mountain
Center

O'Riley looked up from his desk. Dupree stood in his doorway. A surge of adrenaline disrupted the calm rhythm of his heart. "You have something?" If it was another reason they should assume Adam was dead, O'Riley might just snatch the Colt .45 from his middle desk drawer and shoot the depressingly anal-retentive pencil pusher right where he stood.

Dupree flipped through the pages of the status report in his hand as if he needed to quickly review what he was about to say. O'Riley wasn't going to like it, otherwise Dupree wouldn't be stalling.

"The rental car has been recovered."

Damn. "And?"

"The guy who stole it says it was a simple robbery. He and his friends set it up to look as if a woman with a small child had had engine trouble. Apparently they've done this on that particular stretch of road before. The local authorities have been trying to catch them for months." Dupree swallowed hard. "Anyway, a man matching Adam's description stopped to see if he could help and they overtook him."

O'Riley lifted a skeptical brow. "Overtook him?" That was highly unlikely. Enforcers had heightened senses; they weren't easily overtaken.

"The two men had guns," Dupree hastened to explain.

A bad feeling welled in O'Riley's chest. "Did they kill him?"

Dupree shrugged. "We don't know for certain. Apparently, they worked him over pretty good with a tire iron and left him for dead in a ravine. Recon is already on their way to the site. We should know something within the hour."

"Keep me posted," O'Riley said by way of dismissal.

Dupree offered a curt nod and took his leave.

Fury whipped through O'Riley. Every instinct told him that Adam was alive. He glanced at the digital clock on his desk, the one his ex-wife had given him for a divorce present. She'd said it was to remind him of what he'd given up by spending all his time at work. He wondered if anyone would ever know just how much he'd sacrificed. O'Riley leaned back in his chair and banished thoughts of the woman he'd loved and lost. He missed her, that was true enough. But *this* was his life. She hadn't understood that simple fact. He doubted anyone other than the people involved with Center would ever understand. But on days like this he wondered…

He shook off the foolish sentiment—5:05 p.m. He

would have an update on Adam in the next sixty minutes. Between now and then, he had another matter to follow up on—the search for Joseph Marsh, Center's other traitor in all this. Wherever that son of a bitch was, O'Riley wanted him found and executed, after a proper interrogation, of course. Although it had taken someone close to Archer on a personal level to achieve the ultimate goal, O'Riley had a feeling that responsibility for Daniel Archer's death lay squarely on Marsh's shoulders. Why else would Marsh disappear so abruptly?

If Adam were dead, considering what they had so far, they couldn't connect that to Marsh. Still, O'Riley had every intention of seeing that he paid dearly for whatever he had done.

All O'Riley had to do was find him.

Virginia
Archer Ranch

BY DARK that evening, Dani had accomplished more than she had in the past twelve days. Her father's personal belongings were now packed in cedar-lined boxes and stored in his room.

She'd tried to start organizing things the day after he was buried, but she hadn't gotten very far. Fierce emotions would keep her from returning to the task for days at a time. Now, it was finally finished. All that her father had been was now carefully stored away for safekeeping. She couldn't bring herself to donate his clothing. Though he'd had elegant taste and there were surely people who could benefit from his wardrobe, she just couldn't part with anything yet. As long as his things were here, it was as if he might somehow walk through the front door again. As if a part of him remained.

Dani stood in the middle of his study now and wondered if she could handle doing any part of this room today. The last time she'd tried, a couple of days ago, she'd ended up on a crying jag that lasted for hours. Firming her resolve, she surveyed the room. She couldn't fathom any reason to disturb his books. Rich wood shelving lined three walls, leaving room only for the door, while windows that looked out over the grazing pastures, the big red barn right off the pages of a New England calendar and the evergreen mountains beyond lined the fourth. Everything was just as he'd left it.

The books, plaques and awards would stay as they were, she decided. She stared morosely at his antique mahogany desk and the framed photograph that held a place of honor there. She didn't have to pick it up and look at it. She knew it well. It was the last picture taken of her mother. Dani had been ten. They'd gone fishing and she'd caught her first fish. Two days later, her mother was dead.

Fighting back the tears, Dani forced her attention back to the problem at hand. Sorting through his office. She would leave most everything, just not the files. Especially this file. She stared at the odd little electronic storage stick in her hand, still confused by what it contained. She'd never known him to use this sort of storage. The stick was about two inches long and looked like the ones used in digital cameras, which, when inserted into the right plug in one's computer, held the downloaded images captured by the camera. Most of his files were stored on the usual disks and CDs and locked away safely in the basement. He'd ensured that his personal research files from his life's work were properly safeguarded when he retired. Order had been her father's middle name. Everything had its place. But this one file…it just didn't make sense—in more ways than one.

After skirting the large desk, she settled into the soft leather chair and loaded it onto the computer. She'd retrieved it from its original hiding place and brought it into the office with her now to decide what to do with it. She scrolled through a couple of screens that were labeled the Eugenics Project. Like the ones in the basement vault it was encrypted and dated. But unlike the others, which corresponded with the early years of his career, the date on this one was recent. Why would her father have been working on another government program? He was retired. Maybe he'd been consulting? She supposed that was a possibility.

At the funeral, Mr. O'Riley, her father's former director, had said that he hadn't talked to him in months. And her father certainly wouldn't have been discussing a top secret government program with anyone except those with proper clearance. And this project was clearly marked Top Secret. Even stranger, she'd found this odd little file hidden inside the vacuum cleaner. If she hadn't thought the bag was full she would never have opened the canister and checked. The vault in the basement was for safekeeping his work and other personal documents, such as his will, the deed to the property, etc. Why hide this one in the vacuum cleaner, of all places? None of it made sense.

At first, she'd felt certain that he'd put the file there ages ago and forgotten about it. But the creation date on the file, as well as the day and time stamp on the single recorded call on the audiotape, indicated October second of this year, which negated that idea. The file had been stored in its unlikely hiding place the day before her father died. She hadn't found it until three days ago when she'd gone on a cleaning frenzy. Dani had scanned a couple of screens and realized that the information was off limits. She hadn't looked at it again until now—not that she could make head or tail of it anyway since it was encrypted. A couple of times she'd considered calling Mr. O'Riley, but for one reason or another she hadn't gotten around to it.

The audiotape was a minicassette, like the ones used in the dinosaur of an answering machine right here on her father's desk. Her father's personal answering machine, as well as the wall phone in the kitchen, was far from the newest technology.

Dani dragged her fragmented thoughts away from the past and refocused on the tape. Knowing the cryptic call had come in the day before her father's accident made her feel oddly uneasy. The man, whose voice she didn't recognize, had sounded almost frantic. As if on autopilot she put the tape into the machine and pressed the play button to listen to it again now. She didn't know why she tortured herself.

"Archer, call me ASAP. It's extremely important. It's about the Eugenics Project. I think we're in trouble."

The caller had left a number but no name. On impulse, Dani had called the number the first time she'd listened to the tape. She'd gotten a computerized voice mail requesting that she leave a message. She had. She'd informed the caller that her father had passed away, but that she had the file he'd called about if he still wanted it. She left her name and number and suggested that he call her back as soon as possible. After all, she did have a life to get back to, even if she had been putting off making her decision. She recognized that she couldn't stay holed up here forever. It was well past time she finished with the task of settling her father's affairs. And yet, she was still here…putting off what she realized with complete certainty she needed to do.

In the three days since she'd left the message, though, no one had returned her call about the file. Oddly, she'd immediately regretted making that call. The file was marked Top Secret…she wasn't even supposed to have been looking at it. Her father had never involved her in his work. He wouldn't want her involved in it now, but she'd felt compelled to settle all his affairs. She sighed. She didn't want to let him down…not in any way. She hadn't meant to violate security. She had no way of knowing if the caller was even cleared for viewing the file…but then, he'd called it by name. Maybe she was making this harder than it needed to be. She had a responsibility to settle her father's affairs.

Dani picked up the receiver and entered the string of numbers again. The same computerized voice asked her to leave a message. She hung up.

I think we're in trouble.

She'd worked hard not to tack too much significance to that statement. It might not mean anything. But why were the file and the tape hidden in such a manner? If her father hadn't been consulting on a project, then what had he been doing? If she knew the caller's name, that would help. The whole situation was too cloak-and-daggerish.

Dani shoved her fingers into her hair and massaged her aching skull. She did not want to think along those lines. Her father had been a loyal, highly respected civil servant. The sheer number of plaques and certificates in this very room attested to that. He was much loved by his counterparts. She had attended several social functions where he was the man of the hour. His research, though top secret, was, from all indications, unparalleled. She'd been there for his retirement party. Everybody had loved Daniel Archer. There was no reason to believe differently now.

I think we're in trouble.

Why did her instincts have to start plaguing her now? Her father had died two weeks ago. If he'd been involved in anything risky, she would have known it by now. O'Riley would have told her.

What was she thinking? She gave herself a good mental scolding. If her father was involved in a government project, then it was on the up-and-up, end of subject.

Dani started to push away from the desk, but something in her peripheral vision snagged her attention. The final line of text on the screen. *Termination.* A frown tugged at her mouth. The information on the first few screens had been encrypted, but this part wasn't. She scrolled down a little farther. She quickly read the text. It was a report by Joseph Marsh, an old colleague of her father's. She vaguely recognized the name. Why hadn't she looked this far before? She exhaled a weary breath. Because it had been marked Top Secret. Her father had long ago ingrained in her the relevance of security measures. Besides, she had assumed it would all be encrypted.

Uneasiness stirred again in the pit of her stomach as she read the report a second time. It was about an animal training program and its possible termination. But phrases such as *most imperative*, *life-altering* and *frightening consequences* were used. Studying the screen more closely, she decided it was a faxed report her father had scanned into the file. Squinting to make out the tiny print along the edge of the scanned page, she also saw that the sending telephone number was the same as the one on the tape. *I think we're in trouble.* This only confused her further. Was the caller Joseph Marsh? She searched her memory banks in an effort to remember his face or if she'd even met him before. Nothing came to her.

Her first thought when considering animal training was dogs or horses. Was the government using inhumane training procedures? If so, what did it have to do with her father? He was a scientist specializing in human genetic engineering. He didn't train animals.

She stilled. Could her father have discovered that some sort of immoral genetic engineering was taking place using animals? She could definitely see him fighting to ensure the termination of a program he believed was wrong. The frown reached her forehead, etching deep furrows there. If that were the case, he would have gone to any lengths to stop it. He definitely wouldn't have hidden the file or acted in secret. He would have gone straight to O'Riley. Her father had been a strong man. He would never have hidden his beliefs or his actions. Unless…

This couldn't have anything to do with his accident…

Her heart pounded a little harder in her chest. She shook her head. No. That was ludicrous…unthinkable. She wasn't generally the type to think along conspiracy lines.

This couldn't be anything like that. No. It was ridiculous to even consider. She was tired, that's all. The lingering smell of cherry blend pipe tobacco and sandalwood aftershave she'd endured while packing away her father's personal belongings had her nerves raw. She needed something to eat and a long, hot bath. Now that she thought about it, the day had passed without her taking a break. She'd been too upset this morning to eat the muffins she'd gone to the trouble to make…had worked through lunch. No wonder she was so tired. Her body needed fuel.

She quickly closed the file and removed the storage stick from the computer. She started to drop both the stick and the tape into one of the desk drawers, but something she couldn't quite name, a feeling, made her hesitate. Instead, she removed the tape from the machine, turned off the brass lamp and headed into the entry hall. She opened the door to the hall closet and knelt next to the vacuum cleaner. Carefully, she replaced the file and the tape where her father had hidden them.

"This is totally nuts," she chastised herself softly as she got back to her feet and closed the door.

But somehow she felt better knowing it was secured in that way. Her father had hidden it for some reason. And he'd been no fool.

Determined to banish the unsettling thoughts about his last days, Dani turned toward the kitchen. Dinner and then upstairs for a nice long, hot bath. No more sorting and packing. No more conspiracy theories. Tonight, she was going to relax and maybe have a couple of glasses of wine. She might even find an old movie to watch.

And she would forget all about death and conspiracy.

IT WAS dark.

He was cold. Very cold. Pain. He needed to rest, but he was lost. His lids were so heavy he could barely keep his eyes open. The ache in his head pulsed with the beating in his chest.

Light. He could see light from…from a…place. He frowned at his inability to put a name to what he saw. Almost too weak to stand alone, he pushed away from the tree he'd been leaning against and went toward the light.

A long time passed before he reached it. He was so exhausted by the time he got there he wasn't sure if he could go any farther. But he had to get inside…to the light. He would be safer there.

He stared at the door in front of him and tried to think of what to do. He wanted…needed…

He didn't know what…he was tired…so tired.

DANI shivered.

"What is wrong with you, Dani?" She shook her head and took another bite of her sandwich. A heavy silence had invaded the house, or, at least, it somehow felt that way. Despite her best efforts, another shiver danced up her spine one vertebra at a time.

This was ridiculous. She wasn't usually so jumpy.

Unable to help herself, her gaze shiffted to the back door. It wasn't locked. Well, duh. She rarely locked the doors until she went to bed. She tried to ignore the nagging feeling, but it just wouldn't go away. She pushed away from the table, the chair legs scraping over the tiled floor, stood and walked straight to the door and locked it.

"Do you feel better now?" she muttered.

She dropped back into her chair, disgusted with herself. She never acted this way. What was wrong with her? Then it hit her. Rand's hunting story had her spooked. That was it. Dani breathed a much-needed sigh of relief. The tale had been hanging around in the back of her mind and building up panic momentum all day. No wonder she was feeling out of sorts.

If the county had a halfway decent sheriff, she would have called and reported the incident. Though she trusted Rand's and Cal's judgment, she would feel a lot better if someone official checked out their story. But it wouldn't be Sheriff Nichols. She'd already seen more of him than she cared to, and his men were no more welcome on her property than he was. Their allegiance was, of course, to their esteemed leader. She wasn't about to give him a legitimate reason to come around. He might have fooled the locals into voting for him, but Dani knew the pervert behind the badge. How did a guy like him get elevated to a position of such authority? He was a lying, womanizing jerk.

Subject change. She wasn't about to go down that road again. It had taken her months to get over the ulcer she'd developed five summers ago from when that lowlife had attacked her and thought he'd get away with it. She had no intention of working herself up over him now. She was older and wiser.

Unable to finish her sandwich, Dani cleared the table and dropped the remainder of her meal into the trash. It was times like this that made her wish she had a dog. When she felt creeped out, she'd have someone to talk to. Plus, the dog would bark if anyone came around, giving Dani advance notice. But neither she nor her father had ever been able to stay here long enough to justify owning a dog. Finding someone to feed him wouldn't be the problem, but she wouldn't want the poor animal to be lonely.

Since the house sat empty more often than not, that was bound to happen, especially since it was just her now. She doubted she would be able to get back here for more than a few days at a time. She wondered if her father had lived if he'd have eventually gotten a dog. A pet would have kept him company since he'd taken up permanent residence on the ranch after retiring. It was only natural to have a dog in the country, wasn't it? For lots of reasons other than security.

I think we're in trouble.

Dani forced the unbidden thought away. She didn't want to think about that any more tonight. She didn't know what the file was about and there was no reason for her to need to know. Her father had stood steadfastly by that government rule. She never knew anything of his work except on the occasions when he was honored for some undisclosed milestone.

She rinsed her dishes and loaded the dishwasher. There wasn't a full load yet so she opted not to start the cycle. Time for that bath now. Hopefully the hot water would melt away the rest of her tension. The wine she'd had with her meal was already making her feel warm inside.

She poured herself another glass and sipped it

thoughtfully as she walked from the kitchen to the entry hall. The light from the kitchen lit her way well enough that she didn't bother with the hall light. She shifted her glass to her left hand and started unbuttoning her blouse with her right.

If she was lucky, there might be one more envelope of raspberry-scented bath salts. God, that would be heavenly, she thought as she rounded the newel post at the bottom of the stairs.

She stilled when she would have taken the first step up. The hair on the back of her neck stood on end. She swallowed, then turned around slowly. Very slowly.

Someone stood in the shadows shrouding the front door.

Tall. *A man.* Her heart stalled in midbeat.

God, why hadn't she locked the front door? Because no one around here locked doors.

He stepped out of the darkness. The dim glow that reached this end of the hall highlighted the chiseled features of his face. His clothing was torn and disheveled. *Blood.* Dried blood stained the right shoulder of his khaki shirt.

Dani's eyes widened in fear. The urge to scream climbed into her throat.

She had to run. As if he'd read her mind, a strong hand snaked out and manacled her wrist.

She opened her mouth to cry out.

He swayed. She gasped, and then he crumpled to the floor.

Chapter Four

For an endless moment, Dani stood frozen…unable to move or think. Her physician's instincts screamed at her to go to the man who was obviously injured in some way, but the vulnerable, human side of her refused to even breathe, much less move a step in his direction. The skin on her wrist still burned where he had clutched at her so desperately and with such strength. How could a man on the verge of collapsing possess such tremendous strength?

When he continued to lie motionless, those instincts honed for nearly a decade in medical school, then a couple more as a resident, finally kicked in. She crouched next to him, bracing one knee against the smooth hardwood floor.

Her heart racing, she reached toward his throat and the carotid artery there. He was breathing, though his pulse rate was a little slow. Needing more light, she flipped on the overhead fixture and resumed her examination.

His color was ashen. Not good. His clothes were

mud-splattered, with dried leaves stuck here and there in garish decoration. A number of angry scratches marred his face and bare forearms. The dried blood on his shoulder certainly would not have come from any of the scratches. Easing closer, allowing both knees to rest on the floor now, she leaned over him and examined his right shoulder.

The edges of a small tear in the fabric of his shirt were stuck together with blood. As she noted the damage to the khaki material somewhere in the back of her mind she considered that she should be using gloves. Should be calling the police…an ambulance.

She slipped enough buttons from their closures to facilitate sliding the shirt off his shoulder. More red, angry flesh surrounded an already healing circular wound about the size of a nickel. The injury was unmistakable. A bullet wound. Cal's and Rand's story zoomed into her thoughts. But she didn't have time to reflect on that right now.

Using all her strength against the deadweight pressing down onto the floor, she rolled him onto his left side. She carefully peeled the shirt away from his skin to see if the bullet had exited cleanly.

A sigh slipped past her lips when she found the exit wound, larger and not healed quite so well. Okay, there would be no bullet to remove. The incredible fact that the injuries were healed so well eliminated the need for suturing. Allowing his weight to ease back down against the floor, she sat back on her heels and considered her unexpected patient. The gunshot wound wasn't the cause of his current state, that much she'd wager. His flesh felt too warm. She needed to verify his temperature. Maybe an infection?

Proceeding with her examination, she checked his limbs, which appeared to have been working fine before he collapsed. He had moved toward her and his grip had certainly been plenty powerful. All appeared to be in order as she made her way along his lean, muscular limbs and torso, then up his neck. Buried in thick, silky hair, her fingers stilled where they roamed his scalp. There was noticeable swelling at the back of his skull. She rolled him onto his side once more and surveyed the area more closely. The flesh was not damaged or discolored. His full head of blond hair looked no worse for wear. Yet there was a definite raised area.

She had to have help. She couldn't move him on her own. Getting him to the hospital was the next logical step. Calling an ambulance, as she'd considered earlier, would be pointless. By the time it reached her remote location, she could have him at the hospital twice over by herself. She just needed help moving him.

Cal and Rand.

She made the call and in less than fifteen minutes, the two were at her door.

"Holy cow."

Rand looked from the stranger, still unconscious on the floor, to his friend, whose exclamation still echoed in the seemingly too quiet house. "I told you, man," he murmured.

"You think this is the man you saw?" Dani asked as

she knelt next to the stranger and checked his pulse once more. Still a bit slow, but damned steady.

Rand nodded. "It's him." Then he shook his head slowly from side to side in visible regret. "Dammit. I didn't mean—"

"Let's not worry about that right now," Dani interjected. "Help me get him to your truck."

Rand's eyes rounded in terror. "You going to take him to the hospital?"

Cal jabbed him with his elbow. "Of course she is, you idiot. He's been shot."

Dani's gaze locked with Rand's and she knew exactly what he was afraid of. The hospital would be required to report the shooting to the sheriff. Sheriff Lane Nichols was an absolute jerk. The idea of having to deal with him left a bad taste in her mouth as well. She shuddered, then shook off the dread.

"We have to—"

"He's all right, ain't he?" Rand demanded. "I mean, he's not going to die or anything…"

Dani peered down at the stranger once more. "He's stable, if that's what you're asking. His life isn't in danger from the gunshot wound, in my estimation." She considered his heated flesh. Unless an infection was in the works. "But there might be other complications." She shrugged as half a dozen scenarios filtered through her thoughts. "Infection. There's a lump on the back of his skull." She looked up at the boys then. "Could he have fallen after you shot him?"

Both shook their heads vigorously. "He ran like hell,"

Cal explained. "That's why I thought it was a deer. I saw the blood where he'd been hit, but he was long gone."

Rand nodded his agreement. "We weren't close to any bluffs or nothing like that. One second he was there, the next he was gone. I even followed the blood trail for a while but never caught up with him."

"That happens with deer a lot," Cal put in. "That's why I was sure…"

His gaze dropped back down to the man. He didn't have to say the rest. Dani understood. He sincerely thought his friend had shot a deer that had run off to die someplace where his hunters would never locate him.

"If you take him to the hospital," Rand said softly, "the sheriff'll have my hide. He's got it in for me anyway."

Dani could believe that. Nichols had had it in for her for a long time. She didn't trust him. In fact, he scared the hell out of her.

Maybe the boys were right. Maybe involving the sheriff wasn't even necessary. She peered down at the injured man once more. Maybe she could give him all the attention he needed. When he woke up, hopefully she could convince him not to press charges against Rand.

"All right," she said as she pushed to her feet. "Let's get him to the guest room."

The relief on the boys' faces was palpable. She had to be out of her mind. What if something went wrong? What if he took a turn for the worse during the night? Then she'd call that ambulance, she promised herself. But, what if he was a fugitive from the law? For all she knew, he could be a killer. Why else would he hiding out in the woods like that?

Just now taking the time to consider who the guy was, she knelt down next to him and searched his pockets for some sort of identification. His pockets were empty. The possibility that he'd been robbed occurred to her. But why, then, would he hide in the woods?

It didn't make sense.

Any more than what she was about to do.

She stepped back out of the way and let Rand and Cal take over. Cal, the more muscular of the two, hooked his arms under the stranger's and hefted him upward. Rand lifted him with one arm under the bend of each knee. The typical dead man carry.

Moving the stranger didn't actually worry Dani. He'd walked into her home of his own volition, and her examination had given her no reason to believe he had any broken bones. That wasn't to say that there couldn't be fractures undetectable by the naked eye and probing fingers. But that was a risk even paramedics would have to take were they to heft him onto a gurney and into an ambulance.

She followed the slow progress up the stairs. Rand and Cal had to take it one arduous step at a time. The guy was heavy. Dani estimated his height past six feet and his weight close to two hundred pounds. Judging by the fit of his jeans and shirt, every ounce of it was rock-solid muscle.

She swallowed hard as the idea that he could be a fugitive—a rapist or killer—crossed her mind yet again.

Shoving the thought aside, she reminded herself that whoever he was, right now he needed help. Even an inmate on death row received proper medical attention. Now wasn't the time to question her motivation or to second-guess her reasoning. He needed help; she would do what she could.

Once in the upstairs hall, she moved around the three men and hurried to the guest room. She drew back the comforter and top sheet and fluffed the pillows. When Rand and Cal had positioned the injured man on the bed, she removed his hiking boots and set them aside. A frown wriggled its way across her brow as she noted the brand of his shoes. Two hundred bucks minimum. Why would a fugitive from the law be wearing high-priced footwear?

"Help me with his shirt," she said to Cal, who stood on the left side of the bed. Rand stepped out of her way as she moved to the head of the bed.

One quick glance at the label told her that his taste in shirts was every bit as refined as that in his footwear.

When she'd undressed him to the waist she turned to Rand. "Tomorrow morning, I want you up on that mountain. Search the area where you think you saw him and see if you can find a wallet or anything else that might help us identify this guy."

Rand nodded, his eyes still wide with uncertainty. "Does this mean that you're not going to call the sheriff?"

Dani thought about that for a time before answering. "It means," she said carefully, "that I'm going to see

what John Doe here wants to do when he wakes up."
The idea that the lump on his head might be trouble
nagged at her. "But," she warned, looking from Rand
to Cal and back, "if his condition deteriorates in any
way, all bets are off." If hidden trouble existed, symptoms would surface.

The two nodded. "You want us to stay the night,
Miss Dani?" Cal asked.

She decided that was a good idea. "I'd appreciate it.
That way, you'll be close by if I need you."

"We'll call our folks," Rand told her as they left the
room, both looking about ten years older than they had
that morning.

Having them close by would be a good thing. The
house had four bedrooms. There was plenty of space.
At daybreak, she'd send the boys out to search the area
where they thought they'd first encountered this man.
If they could locate the path he'd taken coming down
the mountain, maybe they'd find something. Anything
he'd had in his possession might prove to be useful.

Dani put all other thoughts aside and set to the task
of doing what needed to be done. She gathered the elab-
orate first aid kit she and her father kept at the house
and the necessary cleaning supplies. She also put a call
in to Doc but couldn't reach him. Leaving a message
with his service would work. As soon as he got the
message, he'd call. She needed a second opinion on the
decision she'd made not to go to a hospital right away.

Part of her felt certain she was making a mistake, but
another part of her was convinced that she'd done the

right thing for all concerned. But was the option she'd chosen more right for her and Rand than for this helpless stranger?

After she'd cleaned his wounds and applied topical antibiotic, she determined that his temperature was only slightly above normal. The pupils of his eyes responded appropriately, as did his involuntary reflexes. That puzzled her a bit. The lump on his head and his continued deep sleep made her uncomfortable, but there were no outward symptoms that would dictate concern.

She chewed her bottom lip and thought about the bullet wounds she'd cleansed. According to Rand, the shooting had taken place yesterday morning but the advanced healing indicated otherwise. The wounds should have been still oozing, with scarcely any formation of a scab. Maybe this man's injuries had nothing to do with Cal and Rand.

Her gaze roved over his well-defined torso. He looked to be in excellent physical condition. She was well aware that prisoners had access to state-of-the-art gyms in prison. So his great physical conditioning didn't tell her anything one way or another. His clothes, however, were a different story. How many inmates could afford a single outfit that likely cost five hundred dollars or more? She supposed he could have stolen it, but the fit was perfect. Her gaze moved down the length of his long legs. She didn't have to peel off the denim to clearly see that the rest of his anatomy was as well maintained as his torso.

Another of those foolish shivers danced up her spine

and she chastised herself for being an idiot. She wasn't a kid. Getting caught up in some fantasy here was seriously beneath her. Whatever this man's story, she had to keep her wits about her. Serial killers could be well dressed, even wealthy.

Once she'd covered him with the sheet and comforter, she went downstairs to check on Cal and Rand. Their hushed conversation ceased when she entered the kitchen. The smell of fresh-brewed coffee made her think of long nights at the hospital. She sure hadn't expected to be patching up the wounded tonight.

Cal met her gaze guiltily. "Hope you don't mind that we made some coffee."

"Help yourself to anything you'd like to drink or eat." Supplies needed to be used up, she didn't bother adding. In a few more days, she'd be gone. God only knew how long it would be before she got back here.

"Miss Dani," Rand said, dragging her attention in his direction. His dark hair had fallen into his eyes and he looked suddenly like a child rather than an eighteen-year-old man. "I'm real sorry about all this." He stared at the floor and shook his head. "I didn't mean to cause all this trouble. If that fella—"

"He's going to be fine," she insisted, knowing he needed reassuring. "If there's any permanent damage, it's going to be from the blow he took to the back of his head. The gunshot didn't do any real damage that I can see." She pulled a cup from the cabinet above the coffeemaker. "I don't know his story, but it can't be good." She smiled with as much added reassurance as she could muster. "Whatever his reasons for running around in those woods, they have nothing to do with us. We're helping him. That's a good thing."

"But the sheriff…" Cal's words trailed off.

"Sheriff Nichols is a jerk," she finished for him. "We'll call the state police when the time comes. We're not bothering with that local goofball, agreed?"

The boys nodded, both looking immensely relieved.

It was a damned shame that local law enforcement couldn't be counted on. But it was a cold, hard fact. No way would Dani call them in unless absolutely necessary. It wasn't that the entire department was bad, hardly, but they all answered to one man—Sheriff Nichols.

Dani poured herself a cup of coffee. "I'll sit with him. Keep an eye on his vitals. You two get some sleep. If I need you I'll yell."

When she would have left the room Rand stopped her. "I really appreciate what you're doing for me, Miss Dani."

She looked back at them both and managed another smile. "I'm only doing what my father would have. He considered you two family. Everything's going to be fine."

With that, she headed up the stairs, the mug of coffee warming her cold hands. She'd be lying to herself if she didn't admit that she was worried about her decision. But the memory of almost being raped by the man who wore the sheriff's star in these parts kept her from doing otherwise under the circumstances. Her entire being went stone-cold at the memory.

Still, she was a doctor. This man's life was her first priority. If she thought for one second that her decision would harm him, she would…what? Call the sheriff?

She paused at the top of the stairs and swallowed hard. Would she? Damn, she didn't like feeling this way. She prided herself on helping others. Putting one foot in front of the other, she continued her progress, staunchly putting the what-ifs out of her mind. She would do whatever she had to.

The stranger hadn't moved. He lay just as she'd left him, his respiration slow and deep. She sat down at his bedside and sipped her coffee. That ugly part of her past was something she'd kept carefully locked away for years, but tonight she had no choice but to release it for a few moments.

She'd been only twenty-four and exhausted from her second year of medical school. She'd come home for a desperately needed summer break. Her father had taken a few weeks off work as well. They'd had a wonderful time hiking in the mountains and horseback riding in the meadows. Happiness bloomed in her chest as she thought of the early part of that summer. She'd been so happy. They'd both loved this place so much.

Sheriff Nichols, a deputy at the time, had flirted with her a few times when she'd gone into town for supplies. She'd scarcely had time to even notice the opposite sex the entire year. Her hormones had suddenly awoken with a fury and she'd let the good-looking, smooth-talking deputy woo her into a date. The first time they'd gone out had been nice, really nice. But on the second date, things had changed. The only thing that had saved her from being raped was the course she'd taken in self-defense. He hadn't expected that. Needless to say, her ability to fight back had thoroughly pissed him off.

Dani's heart surged into her throat as the memories tumbled one over the other into her mind. She'd stumbled from his car and run as fast as she could. She'd heard him start the engine to come after her. Every instinct had warned that he intended to hurt her…really hurt her. She'd never seen anyone as angry as he was. But fate had intervened; a passing motorist had stopped and picked her up on the side of the road. She'd watched through the rear window as Deputy Nichols followed behind them. Never once had he offered to stop them or pass them; he had simply followed. When the kindly old man who'd picked her up had dropped her off at her front door, she'd seen Nichols's car waiting out by the main road. He hadn't bothered to approach her house, but he'd watched her go inside.

Her father had been furious and had called the sheriff immediately. The next day the sheriff, as well as Deputy Nichols, had shown up at her home to inform her father that she had lied through her teeth. They even had a witness—one of Lane's friends, of course. Fury boiled up inside her even now. Her father had thrown them out, threatening a lawsuit. But when they'd contacted a lawyer in a nearby town, they'd learned that any attempts to see that the deputy was punished would be futile. The sheriff stood by his men, no matter what.

Now, five years later, Deputy Nichols was the sheriff.

Though she and her father had loved this place, they had known better than to rely on local law enforcement for anything.

Dani set her jaw. No way in hell would she call Sheriff Nichols.

Her gaze settled on the stranger sleeping in her guest bed. If he insisted on calling in the authorities when he woke up, she would cross that bridge when she came to it.

For now, she had only one goal: to keep this guy healthy until she could contact his next of kin.

She just hoped he would let it go at that.

He could very well want more…could demand more.

Only time would tell if luck was going to be on her side.

Chapter Five

"Miss Dani."

Dani looked up to find Cal waiting in the open doorway. She glanced at the stranger still sleeping soundly before pushing out of her chair and joining Cal at the door.

"You sleep all right?" she asked. Even in the dim lighting, she could see the weariness etched across her young friend's face.

He nodded and offered her a cup of coffee.

Grateful, she managed a weary smile. "Thanks." She held the warm mug in her hands and studied his worried expression for a second. "Is Rand holding up all right?" He was the one she was really concerned about.

"He's okay," Cal assured her. "He's waiting down at the truck. I didn't want to leave without letting you know." He flicked a glance at the patient, then looked away just as quickly.

She knew what he meant. He wanted to make sure she was okay before he left her alone with the stranger, sleeping or not. And, a part of him likely still wanted to believe that he'd dreamed all this…that it couldn't be real. But it was. Too damned real.

"I'll be fine, Cal." She placed her hand on his arm and bolstered a genuine smile with as much bravado as she possessed. "You two be careful up there."

He nodded once more, then, with one last lingering look toward the stranger, he left to join his friend outside. Dani shoved her fingers through her hair and sighed. She prayed they would find something to indicate who this man was. If they didn't figure out the mystery soon, they'd have no choice but to contact the authorities. Turning slowly, she sipped the steaming coffee Cal had graciously provided, the familiar scent and flavor of her father's favorite blend somehow comforting.

She stilled as the warm brew slid down her throat. She hadn't thought of him since this began. Her gaze settled on the motionless stranger sleeping in her guest bed. Not once since he collapsed in her entry hall had she thought of her father. Guilt plagued her instantly and the hurt of burying the man she'd loved and respected so very much rushed up into her throat.

God, she missed him so. Nothing would ever be the same without him.

She set her coffee on the bedside table and sat down on the edge of the bed to check her patient's vitals this morning. She'd done so periodically during the night, finding each time that nothing had changed. He slept deeply, his respiration and heart rate remained slow and steady. He'd didn't move, didn't even groan. Any attempts she'd made to rouse him had proven to be futile.

Doc would surely call her this morning. She didn't like this; she needed that second opinion. Her fingers closed around the stranger's wrist and her breath caught at the contact of their skin. His was cool…not overly warm like last night. A frown furrowed her brow. Had his fever passed so quickly? It had been low-grade but still, she'd expected it to worsen, if anything. She'd fully anticipated having to take him to the hospital this morning.

Slipping the thermometer into place, she waited for the beep to confirm her assumption—98.6. She shook her head, bewildered. Maybe she'd misread the thing last night. Perhaps the exertion required to make it to her house had simply elevated his body temperature. Certainly the cool October night hadn't done it. His face abruptly snagged her attention. Her frown deepened as she peered into that handsome face. He was extraordinarily handsome, she realized all over again. Hard jaw…strong brow…nice nose…firm lips. But none of those things held her attention now. It was the scratches.

She drew the covers back from his chest. A gasp escaped her as her brain assimilated what her eyes saw. Every single scratch was almost fully healed, scarcely even visible. Even the bruises had faded to practically nothing. The gunshot wound looked weeks, rather than days, old.

This was impossible.

Pushing her hands between his head and the pillow, she slowly, carefully probed the back of his skull. Another shock quaked through her. The lump she'd worried about last night was all but gone.

She suddenly wished Rand and Cal were still in the house. They'd gotten a good look at the guy. They would remember the scratches and the wound on his shoulder. Surely she hadn't imagined the severity of the injuries.

Caffeine. She needed more caffeine to bring her up to speed with the thoughts whirling inside her head. She eased back into her chair and downed the still-warm brew in a few gulps.

She'd read about rapid healers, even run across one or two as a resident. The concept wasn't unheard of, but she'd never read or even heard about anything like this. She'd certainly never seen anyone heal practically overnight. Shaking her head again, she told herself that there had to be some sort of explanation. She glanced at the clock. It was 8:00 a.m. already. Where was Doc? He'd been in the business of caring for the sick and injured a whole lifetime. Maybe he'd seen something like this before.

Dani stilled. Perhaps mentioning the rapid change wasn't such a good idea. As much as she loved Doc, he had worried about her the past couple of weeks. He'd suggested more than once that the strain of losing her father had taken a heavy toll on her. That was true. But she sensed that he meant a good deal more than what she did. She couldn't help feeling that he was somehow insinuating that she'd slipped over some precipice. Dani bit her lower lip and thought about that for a bit. For as long as she could remember, Doc had been like a brother to her father, very much like an uncle to her. But his worry seemed misplaced somehow…almost as if he expected her to fall apart.

She shrugged. Maybe he did. He missed her father, too. Perhaps he needed to feel needed. She'd always been strong. Well, except that one summer. A shudder rumbled through her as thoughts of the sheriff flickered across her mind. She'd almost lost it that summer. Her father and Doc had seriously worried over her seeming inability to pull it back together after that. But she'd managed. She'd gone back to med school and thrown herself into her studies. Who needed a social life anyway? Hadn't she discovered firsthand just how much trouble one could be?

Unfortunately, that's the way it had been ever since. Not that she didn't date occasionally. She'd even had a relationship or two. But nothing ever lasted. Was her inability to commit the sheriff's doing as well? She imagined a psychiatrist would say so. She'd done a rotation in psychology. The idea that she purposely steered clear of relationships and commitments was not lost on her.

Her attention returned to the man sleeping a few feet away. No. Maybe she wouldn't mention his vast improvement to Doc. She had no desire to rouse his overprotective side even further. Whoever this John Doe was, she had to get him back on his feet and somehow attempt to dissuade him from ruining Rand's life. The kid had made a mistake—a bad one, but a mistake nonetheless. He was a good guy. He deserved a second chance.

She watched the rhythmic rise and fall of the man's chest and let go a weary sigh. Please, Lord, she prayed, just let this one be a good guy as well.

Ghost Mountain
Center

O'RILEY SAT for a long moment after Dupree had given him the latest update on the Adam situation. His body had not been found in the ravine, although, during the past twelve hours, DNA testing had confirmed that trace evidence—a couple of hairs and a few slivers of skin—found at the scene did belong to Adam.

He had been there.

He'd either walked away or had been carried.

Additional interrogation of the thieves who had ambushed him had yielded nothing. They had left him in the ravine. End of story.

O'Riley ran a weary hand over his face. Damn, he was tired. He hadn't left Center in more than forty-eight hours. Hadn't slept in the same. If this was about more than a simple robbery…

He shook off the thought, unprepared for that scenario just yet.

"The reconnaissance team won't stop searching until they've covered one hundred square miles around the ravine," Dupree said, drawing his attention back to the here and now. "As per your instructions, they're questioning everyone in the area, including local law enforcement."

O'Riley didn't like involving the locals but, unfortunately, it was necessary. He couldn't risk Adam slipping through the cracks.

"He hasn't turned up at any of the hospitals or clinics?" If Adam were injured, and he assuredly was, he would seek help. Unless, of course, those injuries somehow involved his cognitive ability. O'Riley didn't want to dwell on that train of thought. Adam was the very best of the Enforcers. They couldn't afford to lose him. Not with the senate hearings coming up. They needed him to prove their worth when it came time for funding.

Dammit all to hell. He would kill Marsh with his bare hands when he found him. The son of a bitch had certainly set all this in motion. Thurlo would never have had the guts alone. O'Riley had every intention of seeing that the bastard lived to regret it.

"He hasn't shown up at any of the hospitals or clinics," Dupree droned on in answer to O'Riley's question. "That is, assuming he isn't dead and yet to be identified."

O'Riley slammed his fists down on top of his desk. Dupree jumped, then straightened his glasses. "We're not going to consider that possibility," O'Riley warned, "until all others are exhausted. Do I make myself clear?" How many times did he have to tell the man?

"Yes, sir. O-of course." Dupree cleared his throat. "Another option we need to…" He swallowed hard. "We need to consider is that he could have neurological damage from the repeated blows to the head."

The bastard who'd put Adam down had admitted that he'd beaten him repeatedly with the tire iron even after rendering him unconscious. O'Riley gritted his teeth. That could explain the malfunction in the tracking device. Its location at the base of Adam's skull would make it vulnerable to that type of blow.

"What does Medical have to say about that?" Medical encompassed the entire department of human physical and mental research at Center. It was the staff's job to know everything about the human body and mind. Numerous other departments focused on their own fields of research, such as the Eugenics Department that focused solely on the enhancement of human creation. Then there was the Preservation Department that, as one would guess, concentrated on extending life. There was a department for everything around here. And at the head of each was a certified genius, with dozens of others of the same caliber working beneath him or her.

With that many great minds walking around, was it too much to ask to find one damned man?

"The blows could explain the malfunction of the TD," Dupree rambled on.

O'Riley rolled his eyes. "Now tell me something I don't already know."

Dupree cleared his throat again and shifted uncomfortably in his chair. "It's possible there could be damage to his ability to process thought, to reason. That would explain why he hasn't tried to contact Center. He may simply be wandering aimlessly."

O'Riley pressed Dupree with a gaze he hoped conveyed the full import of what he was about to say. "I want him found. Dead or alive. I want him back here within forty-eight hours. Do you understand me, Dupree?"

He nodded stiffly. "Yes, sir." He pushed to his feet.

"I'll advise the team to intensify the search. Shall we organize a backup team to finish Adam's mission?"

The mission.

There was still that. He shook his head. "Not just yet. Dani Archer isn't going anywhere right now. We have time."

Dupree nodded and scurried away.

O'Riley leaned back in his chair and shook his head. They didn't need this complication right now. An election year was upon them. The race was going to be so damned close that any little thing could tip the balance. If their man failed to hang on to the presidency, they might just be finished. Though Center was supported by a number of foreign allies, they couldn't survive without full support from the president of the United States. Besides, their first allegiance was always with their own country. O'Riley had no intention of allowing that to change. Protecting Center was priority one.

No one, not Adam, not even the future president, was more important than seeing that their mission continued. The work at Center was the future of this great nation.

The future of mankind…period.

"WE DIDN'T FIND anything," Rand repeated.

Dani couldn't help feeling disappointed. She had really hoped that they would find a wallet, at least a driver's license that would tell them who their John Doe was. She tamped down the disappointment and assumed a hopeful face for Rand's sake. He was taking all this damned hard.

"That's all right, Rand," she insisted. "I'm sure he'll wake up soon and then we'll know."

Neither of the boys looked reassured.

"I know you two have jobs to get to," she hastened to add. "I'll call if there's any news." Cal and Rand worked for Rand's father on his horse ranch. They were likely late already.

"We'll stop by after work," Cal said. "We've fed the horses. We'll go ahead and do that from now on. Call if you need us."

"Don't worry, I will." She followed them to the front door, part of her feeling reluctant to let them go. Maybe being alone with the stranger upstairs wasn't such a good idea. But what choice did she have? They had to get to work and Doc still hadn't called. Neither of those things mattered; she was only being silly. The stranger was in no condition to be a threat.

"Miss Dani, I—" Rand stared down at the wooden floor of the front porch, whatever he'd been going to say stuck in his throat.

"It'll be okay, Rand." She patted him on the shoulder. "Go on to work and don't worry about this. I've got it under control."

He nodded and trudged off toward his truck, Cal at his side. Dani suddenly wished for a friend like that. She wondered if Rand knew just how lucky he was. Though she'd had her share of friends, she'd never had one she could call a best friend. With the private schools she'd attended, there had been too big a turnover in the enrollment. A friend's father or mother was always getting transferred to some other government appointment. Not many ever stayed more than a year or two. With the few who did, they would lose touch during the summer since Dani and her father always came back to the ranch for vacations. Every fall, it had been like starting over. Each time, someone new had always appeared who had proven to be more interesting or more outgoing than her and Dani had been passed over by her friends for the new girl in the class.

Oh well, that had been a long time ago. Admittedly, things hadn't changed much in her adult life, mainly because she didn't have time for friends who were that close.

Or relationships, she mused with self-deprecation.

"Pathetic, Archer," she muttered. "Truly pathetic."

Before she went back upstairs to check on her patient, she made herself a piece of toast and washed it down with some orange juice. When she headed for the stairs once more, she considered that maybe she should try to rouse the patient again. She'd tried several times during the night with no success. That part worried her. It was almost as if he'd slipped into a coma so his body could heal. It happened. With the speed at which this guy had healed, whatever his body was doing, it was definitely working.

The telephone rang when she would have taken the first step up the stairs. She rounded the newel post and snatched up the receiver from the unit on the entry hall table.

"Hello."

"Dani, it's Doc. Is everything all right?"

She suddenly questioned the judiciousness of dragging him into this.

"Well." She glanced toward the second-story landing. "I…" For the first time in her life she hesitated about telling Doc the truth. She'd always been straight with her father and Doc. They'd always treated her as an equal, never as a child. Why the hesitation now? If she'd made a mistake, would Doc be held liable as well?

"Everything's okay," she lied. "I just…needed to hear your voice." Dammit, why did she lie? To protect him or herself?

"You packed your father's things," he guessed. He knew her so well.

She blinked back the tears and took a deep, cleansing breath. "Yes."

"Would you like me to take you out to dinner tonight? Get you away from the house for a while?"

She glanced up the stairs once more. "That sounds great, but I…I promised Rand and Cal I'd have dinner with them tonight." She hated herself for lying to him, but she couldn't leave her patient. She imagined Rand and Cal would be joining her.

"Ah…they've started preparing for hunting season already," Doc guessed again. Damn, did nothing escape the man's notice? Though he had no idea about the injured man, he'd sure nailed down everything else that was going on in her life.

"They started a couple of days ago," she agreed. She wondered if hunting season would ever be the same for them after this. She had the sudden, almost overwhelming sensation that nothing would. She forced the eerie feeling away. Her emotions were still raw from losing her father, that's all. Add to that this stranger's appearance and the circumstances that had brought him to her and she had a right to feel anxious and unsettled.

"Well, I've got dozens of messages to return, so I'll let you go. Call me if you need anything at all," he said kindly.

"Thanks, Doc."

When they'd said their goodbyes Dani replaced the receiver in its cradle and trudged up the stairs feeling like the scum of the earth. How did she propose to keep this a secret? She should simply have told Doc the truth. When he found out—and he would find out—he would really think she'd gone over the edge.

Who knew? Maybe she had.

After all, she was harboring what could be a fugitive from justice in her guest room. Not to mention he could very well be in a coma. If that were the case, her actions weren't harming him further but she had behaved unprofessionally. Were his head injury, assuming he had one, more severe than she believed, she would know it by now. His pupils would not react to light properly and there would be other outward indications, such as seizures. Her delay in reporting him to the local authorities or in taking him to the hospital was not going to endanger him, she told herself again. He was…

Her next thought evaporated as her gaze settled on the guest room bed.

He was gone.

Fear, stark and vivid, slammed into her gut.

The covers lay in a tangled mass on the floor. Thank God the windows were still closed. The bathroom. Her gaze flew to the open door leading to the adjoining bathroom. It was the Jack-and-Jill type that connected this bedroom to another. Maybe he'd slipped out of the room that way. Or maybe—

Her thought abruptly ceased as she was yanked backward by the hair of her head. She shrieked, tried to twist away but a strong arm banded around her waist and jerked her against what felt like a brick wall.

Him.

He didn't have to speak. She recognized his strength…the touch of his hand.

"I'm trying to help you," she said softly, urgently.

His hold on her tightened, drawing her harder against his muscular body. His fingers twisted in her hair and she couldn't help but cry out with the pain of it.

"Please," she whispered. "Don't hurt me. I want to help you. You've been hurt. I'm a doctor."

His hold on her loosened and it was all she could do not to bolt away from him, but that would be a mistake, she sensed. Slowly, careful not to make any sudden moves, she turned to face him. His fingers were still tangled loosely in her hair. The fingers of his other hand never lost contact with her body, but he allowed her to turn, to look up at him.

"I'm glad you're awake," she told him carefully. "Can you tell me your name?"

He stared at her with such intensity that goose bumps prickled her skin. Those blue eyes were like none she had ever seen. The most unique blend of sea and sky. The features of his face were grim, his color no longer ashen. How could he have recovered so quickly?

He opened his mouth, but no sound came out. Then he snapped it shut once more, something like frustration overtaking his expression.

She reached for the hand in her hair and pulled it away so that she could check his pulse. He watched intently as she calculated the rate. "Good," she said. Strong, steady, and not nearly so slow as last night.

Motioning toward the bed she urged, "Let's sit down."

He allowed her to lead him to the bed. She sat down on the edge of the mattress and after a few seconds, he did the same.

She wasn't sure how he would react to her next move. She needed to know that his heart was beating properly and without a stethoscope, she had only one option. She lowered her head toward his chest, but he moved away.

She fixed her gaze on his and held it for several moments. "It's okay," she soothed. "I won't hurt you." When the tension in his muscles had relaxed, she leaned down once more. She pressed her ear to his chest and listened. His heartbeat was strong and steady, no anomalies whatsoever that she could hear. His flesh felt warm against her cheek. A stir of something completely unprofessional made her breath catch. Before she could analyze her reaction to feeling his skin against her cheek, his fingers had delved into her hair again and he'd drawn her face away from him.

"It's good," she said with as much reassurance as she could marshal with him staring at her so fiercely. Part of her was scared to death but the other part, some feminine side she scarcely recognized, felt something along the lines of anticipation. How crazy was that?

She froze, her breath stalling in her throat once more as he lowered his head to her chest, mimicking her actions. He pressed his ear against her and held perfectly still just as she had done. Her heart thundered in her ears and heat rushed through her veins. It was totally ridiculous, yet she couldn't control the sensation.

He lifted his head and looked down at her no doubt helpless expression and said, "Good."

His voice was rough, deep, like velvet sliding over gravel. She got the distinct impression the word was more an echo of hers than a statement of his conclusion. But that would mean…that couldn't be. If his head injury were severe enough to cause that kind of damage, he'd likely be dead now or in a deep coma.

With no other recourse, she nodded her understanding. "Good."

Forcing herself to think like a doctor rather than a woman, she considered that he was probably dehydrated. "I'm sure you're thirsty and hungry," she said more to herself than to him. She reached for the glass of water she'd kept on the bedside table just in case he awoke and needed it. She offered it to him. "You should try and drink this."

He stared at the glass, then at her.

Oh, Lord. This was bad. He didn't appear to under-stand what to do.

She moved the glass toward his lips and he drew away. Her heart skipped a beat. Oh, damn. Wait, she told herself, calming to some degree. This might have noth-ing to do with his injuries. He could be a fugitive from some sort of hospital or home. He might be cognitively deficient. She looked at that sculpted chest and won-dered how someone incapable of feeding himself could hone his body to such perfection.

It didn't make sense.

Knowing he needed to drink, she did the only thing she knew to do since she didn't have an IV handy to pump fluids into his veins, assuming he'd let her near him with a needle. She sipped the water. "Hmmm. Good."

He looked at her mouth, then at the glass. Moving slowly, she offered the glass to him again, holding it close to his mouth. Hesitantly, he allowed his lips to touch the rim. She watched in startled fascination as he took a tiny sip. His lips were full and firm. She rolled her eyes at the thought. What was she doing admiring his mouth? As soon as his senses identified the water as a good thing, he wrapped his hands around hers and turned the glass upward. He drank deeply, allowing water to dribble down his chin and throat.

"Whoa," she warned. "Slow down a little." But it was too late. The water was gone. Unable to halt the instinct, she swiped his chin and throat with her hand. A sizzle of flat-out lust shook her as her palm smoothed over the warm, male flesh. What was wrong with her? This man could be a mental patient for all she knew!

He looked at the empty glass in her other hand and murmured, "Good."

She gave herself a mental kick. He needed her help. He was thirsty, most likely hungry and needed a bath and clean clothes. Whatever lapse in judgment she'd suffered moments ago was inconsequential. She was a doctor and he needed her.

His needs were all that mattered at the moment.

At least now she knew one thing for certain—she was completely safe with this man. He was as harmless as a child.

Her gaze swept over him once more before she could stop it. She resisted the urge to shake her head. He damn sure didn't look harmless.

He looked…dangerous.

Chapter Six

He ate cereal. He ate two sandwiches. Whatever she put in front of him, he ate it…but only after she showed him how to proceed.

Dani chewed her lip and watched the stranger consume another bowl of cereal. His table manners left a lot to be desired. But there was just something incredibly moving about watching a half-naked man devour his food more with his fingers than with a spoon.

The way he mimicked her words nagged at her as well. Like a child…only with a much deeper voice. She shivered when she thought of the sound. Deep, rough, sexy. She blinked, startled that she'd let that last word slip into her assessment. What was wrong with her that she couldn't seem to keep her mind off sex? Her life was in an emotional tailspin just now. She should understand; it was as basic as biology got. She craved any sort of bonding to comfort herself.

She squared her shoulders and forced her attention back to the matter at hand. She'd tried a phrase in every language she knew and even some she'd only picked up from movies. Spanish, French, Italian…even a word or two of Russian. He'd only looked at her much like her horse did when she did something the animal didn't comprehend. Those intense blue eyes of his just bored right into her as if he were attempting to see inside her head.

The bowl clattered to the table. She jumped as if a shot had been fired. Her gaze locked with the stranger's and he said, "Good."

Dani shook her head and scrubbed a hand over her face. This was way out of her league. She should have told Doc when he called. She needed help here. Another thought occurred to her. Maybe she'd take him to Doc's clinic. Whatever he needed for the examination would be there. As she pushed herself to her feet, the idea gelled fully. That was the right course of action. She looked down at her patient, who was staring up at her like an obedient puppy waiting for the next command.

A sigh hissed past her lips as she gazed into that handsome face. What woman wouldn't give her eye-teeth to have a guy like this staring up at her in just this manner? She shook herself again…something she was doing a lot of today. Get him ready to see Doc. That was the plan.

She took his hand and tugged. He stood, his chair scraping across the floor, and followed without hesitation. On the way up the stairs, she considered the issue of clothing. His shirt was ruined, but his jeans would survive but had to be laundered. She could handle that. He was too large, especially across the shoulders, to wear anything that had belonged to her father. Maybe a T-shirt would stretch enough to fit. Over the years, her father had kept every T-shirt she'd bought him with silly sayings like Genius At Work or Man Of The Year. One of those would do. But first, she had to get this guy into the shower.

She led him into the guest bath adjoining the room where he'd slept. It always took a couple of minutes for the water to warm up so she turned it on and used the intervening time to gather a towel and a fresh bar of soap. When she'd stationed both in the shower, she turned to John. She couldn't keep calling him the stranger or the patient. She blinked. Not until that second had she considered that his clothes would need to come off for the shower. Great.

Nor had she considered how he would react to the spray of water. She swore softly.

"Dammit."

She looked up at the harshly uttered word, then laughed. He had repeated her curse. She frowned, but she'd uttered it so softly. How had he heard it over the sound of the water in the shower? Well, at least she knew his hearing was up to par.

After opening the shower door, she reached inside and allowed the water to spray over her arm. "Good," she said to him. This was the one word he seemed to understand.

Slowly, looking from the shower to her and back, he reached inside and did the same. "Good," he echoed.

Well, that was a start. She dried her hand and went

for broke. "Okay, John, I know you're not going to understand this, but we need to remove your jeans."

He watched her lips as she spoke, which did strange things to her equilibrium. Forcing the sensations to the back of her mind, she reached for the snap of his jeans. She'd seen hundreds of patients naked, male and female. This would be no different. When she'd unfastened the jeans, she took his hands and helped him to push them down slightly. He just stared at her, confusion marring that perfect face.

"Look," she said, frustrated, "we have to get your jeans off." She pushed the waistband a little lower. The stretchy boxer briefs he wore beneath went down, too. Though he didn't resist, he made no move to assist her efforts. "Good," she suggested in hopes of encouraging his participation.

A split second before she saw it coming, he reached for the button at the waist of her jeans. "No." She pulled his hands away, urging him to remove his own jeans.

It went on this way for a minute or so before he seemed to get her intent. Finally, his muddy jeans lay in a heap on the floor along with his navy boxer briefs. She gestured to the shower. "Time to get inside," she urged.

Again, he simply looked at her while she struggled with the urge to visually scrutinize the rest of his body. She refused to allow it, of course, but the urge was very nearly overpowering all the same.

"John." She took his face in her hands, drawing his full attention to hers. The feel of his beard-stubbled cheeks made her shiver. "Get in the shower." She turned his head until he was looking into the shower, then she gave him a little push in that direction. He resisted at first, but then he stepped inside as if he'd decided it was the right thing to do. "Thank God," she muttered. Before the words were scarcely out of her mouth, he'd grabbed her by the arm and yanked her into the tiled cubicle with him.

He stared down at her, the water sluicing over his shoulders, like a golden Adonis beneath an unexpected rain straight from Zeus. "Good," he murmured.

Why the hell not? "Good," she agreed.

Dani learned one very important lesson from that shower, it didn't matter how many nude bodies she'd encountered during the course of her medical training, how many male specimens she'd examined from head to toe as a physician, it was still more than merely possible to be totally amazed. John Doe was beautiful in every respect. From his full head of blond hair to his well-formed feet, he was perfect. And though she was fully clothed, he had rubbed soap all over the damp fabric she wore just as she had over his smooth, wet skin.

A lesson in shaving came next. The removal of several days' beard growth only made him more handsome. No man should look that good.

Noon had come and gone by the time she had him back in his freshly laundered briefs and jeans. The Genius At Work T-shirt was stretched like a second skin over his upper torso. She'd called Doc's clinic and gotten his nurse to divulge the time he planned to take a short break. Now all she had to do was get John there.

With his shoes tied and his hair brushed, he looked nothing like the man who'd stumbled into her entry hall last night. His color was tanned and healthy. Despite being blond, he had the kind of coloring that looked suntanned all year round. During the teeth-brushing session she'd noted that all his teeth were there and, like everything else about him, were movie star quality.

As they exited the house, she hesitated. For the first time since she'd decided to take him into town, she realized that she'd have to drive her father's car. Her gaze went instantly to the detached garage. She'd flown here just over two weeks ago, frantic and in a near state of shock. She'd scarcely remembered to bring her purse. She hadn't bothered with a rental car, hadn't brought her medical bag—which she usually took everywhere with her. Her whole life had turned upside down with that one call from Doc.

Dani…it's your father. There's no other way to say this, sweetheart. He's dead.

Tears welled before she could stop them. She blinked frantically. She didn't want to cry anymore. "Wait here," she said to John. She had to have the keys. They couldn't go anywhere without the keys.

She hurried back into the house. She remembered seeing his keys on his desk. It was hard to believe she'd been here over two weeks and hadn't left the place other than for the funeral service and burial. Cal, Rand and Doc had brought her anything she'd needed.

Holding her breath, she snatched up the keys and headed back to the front door. What she found in the entry hall brought her up short and sent the breath she'd been holding clean out of her lungs in a rush.

John stood there, a framed photograph of her and her father clutched in his hands. He stared at it so intently that she trembled at the sight. As she watched, he touched the face of Daniel Archer in the photograph, an indefinable emotion moving across his. "Good," he whispered.

A fresh wave of tears came out of nowhere and Dani scarcely forced them back. "We should go." She took the photo from him and placed it back on the hall table next to the telephone. "Come on." For one long beat, he stared at her and she could have sworn that he recognized her somehow, but that was impossible.

"Come on, John."

Thirty minutes later, they were waiting in Doc's private office. The room was much like her father's study back at the house. Paneled walls lined with shelves. Only Doc's shelves were filled with ancient medical tomes related to the practicing physician. She smiled, thinking how she'd loved to look at those books as a child. She could sit for hours behind his desk perusing one volume after the other. He was the whole reason she'd become a practicing physician when her father would have loved nothing better than for her to go into research as he had.

Just like in her father's study, the large ashtray held a place of honor along with a favorite pipe and a tin of cherry tobacco. A wool cardigan hung in the corner behind his desk. God, how she had loved this office. She'd played here for hours when her father had had a meeting back in Washington that he hadn't been able to put off. Doc had always been happy to keep her entertained for the day. On slow days, he'd even had her help with the patients. How could she have grown up to become anything but a doctor?

John sat statue still in one of the chairs flanking the Doc's desk. He simply watched her move about. His vocabulary had already increased considerably. *Good* was no longer his only means of communication. He now understood no, yes, and more than a dozen other words like car, keys. Just in the past hour or so. She didn't understand how he could catch on so quickly when he seemingly had no knowledge of the object prior to her introducing him to it. The whole concept was too bizarre.

The door opened and Nurse Keller stuck her head into the office. "He's almost ready."

"Thank you." Dani produced a smile for her. When she'd closed the door once more, Dani looked directly at John to make sure he was listening to her. "I'll be right back."

Whether he understood or not, she couldn't be sure, but he made no move to follow her. She stepped into the corridor outside the office just as Doc headed that way. She needed a few minutes of privacy before he met John. She wasn't sure discussing her concerns regarding his case in front of him was a good idea.

"What a pleasant surprise!" Doc hugged her. "It's wonderful to see you out and about, Dani."

She inhaled the scent of him, a hint of some springy bath soap as well as the heavier smell of disinfectant used in all clinics and hospitals. Both were underscored by the vaguest hint of cherry pipe tobacco. He smelled like Doc, like home and family, and she was so glad to be in his arms. She suppressed the urge to cry again before she drew back to look into those caring eyes behind the thick lenses of his eyeglasses.

"It's good to be out," she confessed, then took a deep, bolstering breath. "I know I've got to get on with my life. It's what he would want."

Doc nodded a gesture of surety. "You're absolutely right. Your father would never in a million years want you to put anything on hold for him. So, when are you heading back to the West Coast?"

The question startled her for a moment, but then she grasped his intent and smiled. Going back to work was part of getting on with her life. "I promised Dr. Feldon I'd be back a week from Monday." It was Wednesday already. A week from Monday suddenly seemed too soon. But it was the right thing to do.

The idea that John Doe waited on the other side of the door suddenly pushed all else aside. "I…" She squeezed Doc's arms before letting go. "I have a problem."

His brow furrowed with concern. "Oh?"

"Join me in your office."

Dani had expected to find John waiting right where

she'd left him. But he surprised her. As she had done dozens of times as a young girl, he stood next to row after row of book-lined shelves, a heavy volume in his hands, his head bowed in deep concentration.

John had appeared nervous when she brought him into the clinic. He'd been particularly determined not to let Nurse Keller touch him, but with Doc he was downright combative. He had no intention of allowing the older man near him.

When Dani had finally settled him back into his chair, she explained the previous night's events to Doc.

Doc sat down behind his desk and picked up his pipe. He wouldn't light it in her presence since, like her father, he wasn't supposed to indulge in that habit any longer, but he would stroke it lovingly and would partake of the forbidden indulgence the moment he had some time alone. She couldn't prevent a tiny smile. He and her father had been friends for so long they'd picked up each other's habits, or maybe they'd picked up those habits together along the way. A part of her father was still alive in Doc, and she cherished that connection.

"You say there was a lump last night? The back of his skull?" Doc inquired.

"Yes." Oddly, when she'd helped him wash his hair this morning it had disappeared entirely. "But it's gone now."

Doc's frown deepened. "He mimics your words and actions?"

She nodded. "Like a child, only a lot faster."

"What about reading?"

They both looked at the volume John had been holding when they'd entered the office. "I don't know," Dani said slowly. She reached for the book, flipped it open and before she could comment further, John quoted an entire paragraph from the preface of *Gray's Anatomy*. She and Doc exchanged startled looks.

"Well, I guess he answered that question," Doc suggested.

Dani set the book aside and shrugged. "What do you think?"

Doc studied John for a time. John returned his analyzing gaze with a searching one of his own. "I could examine him but I don't see the point in agitating him. I wouldn't pick up on anything you haven't already."

Dani almost argued the point with him. She, after all, had conducted her examination without the aide of medical instruments.

"I would recommend that he see a neurologist. There are a couple of mental disorders that allow for such exact mimicking, but the fact that you had to show him how to feed himself points in another direction entirely."

"Global amnesia," Dani offered.

Doc nodded. "But the kind of physical trauma necessary to induce that level of amnesia doesn't fit with his obvious state of excellent health. Still, the neurologist could do a scan to see if there has been neurological trauma at some earlier date. Perhaps he was injured and—" Doc waved his arms magnanimously "—somehow survived in the woods like an animal." He settled his gaze on Dani. "You may be his first human contact since the trauma. But that's a stretch. On the other hand, the concept of emotional trauma doesn't fit, since his memory loss extends to motor skills."

She agreed. "Who would you recommend?" Getting John to a neurologist was the right thing to do.

Doc flipped through his Rolodex. "Let's go with Carl Nevin. He's excellent."

As Doc put in a call to Nevin's office, Dani considered the other thing it appeared she would have to do: contact the police. Since John didn't know who he was, it was her duty to attempt to find out. There could be a missing person's report that would identify him. Fingerprints. Or, for all she knew, an APB if he were a fugitive from the law.

"Tomorrow morning at ten okay with you?" Doc asked her as he turned the receiver into his shoulder. She nodded and he made the final arrangements. When he'd jotted down the address of the office in nearby Richmond, he passed it across the desk to her.

"I assume you're going to the police next."

Dani could tell by his somber tone that he knew she didn't want to do that, but he also knew that she wasn't foolish enough to think there was any way around it.

"I guess I don't have a choice. I can't just take him in like a stray puppy. He may have a wife and family looking for him." The idea of a wife jolted her unreasonably. She pushed away the foolish reaction and focused on what Doc was saying.

"I know how you feel about Sheriff Nichols. How

about we call a friend of mine who works with the Virginia State Police over in Richmond. He'll have access to all the necessary systems and you can trust him. Maybe he can see you tomorrow as well."

Relief came in a rush. "That would be great." Even the idea of having to face Lane Nichols made her want to cringe. Putting aside their ugly past, she wasn't at all sure she could trust the man to do his job. She would never understand how he got himself elected. Obviously he'd fooled the whole county.

Dani thanked Doc and led John back to her car. He fastened his seat belt without her having to instruct him. She couldn't get over what a quick learner he was. Amazing. Neither could she wait to hear the neurologist's conclusions. Every instinct told her that John was special. She looked over at him just in time to see him pick up the Virginia road map her father kept lying on the console. He unfolded the map and studied it as if he knew exactly what he was doing. As she braked for a traffic light, Dani wondered what it was that this man did for a living. Who was he? Where had he come from? Was there a wife and children? A fiancée or girlfriend? Brothers? Sisters?

She shook her head and turned her attention back to the street. Whoever John Doe was, he wouldn't be with her long. Tomorrow, once she'd contacted the investigator Doc had recommended from the Virginia State Police, he would enter John's description and prints into one or more systems and a name would pop out and John would be taken away. The feeling of emptiness that accompanied that thought made her want to kick herself. How in the world had she gotten so attached to the man so quickly? She had to remind herself again that she'd just lost her father. She needed something— anything—to grab on to.

It just happened to be this John Doe.

DINNER THAT NIGHT turned into a game. John decided that turnabout was fair play. If Dani could feed him, he could feed her. She was certain he hadn't meant for the game to be sensual. He was like a child…innocent. Which made her ridiculous feelings of attraction to him kind of sick. But she just couldn't help herself.

She'd left him in her father's den, fascinated with the news channel, while she cleaned up the kitchen. With him occupied, she'd called Cal and then Rand to let them know the latest news. Both were relieved to hear from her, Rand especially. He had come over that after- noon and looked after the horses. She'd told them she would take care of the horses as long as she was in town, but now she was glad they'd taken that worry from her. She just hadn't the energy left to deal with anything else.

When the kitchen was taken care of she returned to the den to find it empty. The television was still on, but John was nowhere to be found. Her heart surged into her throat. What if he'd gone outside? If he got lost in the mountains again, anything could happen to him. He was helpless!

She rushed toward the front door only to come to a

grinding halt at the entrance to the entry hall. John stood by the console table staring at a silver-framed picture of her father. He studied it so intently that she hesitated to interrupt him. This was twice now she'd found him this way. Was it possible that he knew her father somehow? She didn't see how that was possible. Maybe her father reminded him of someone in his life. Perhaps staring at the images of her father was helping to bring back his real memories—assuming it was possible to recoup any. From what she recalled about global amnesia, the chances of recovering lost memories were highly unlikely. The brain damage was usually too severe. But there was always the exception.

If there ever lived an exception, Dani had a feeling John would be one.

"That's my father," she said aloud, making her presence known.

He looked up sharply, his muscles tensing instantly as if he'd gone on guard. She wondered at that, too. Whenever she caught him by surprise, he tensed visibly. Was that part of the result of his injury or residual from his prior life?

She had no way of knowing. As he watched her, which he did quite a lot, she moved toward him. "Daniel Archer," she explained and pointed to the man in the photograph he held. "That's my father."

John studied the face she'd pointed to, then looked at her. "Good," he said.

He'd done that before. This morning. Again she had that feeling that he somehow knew her father. But that was ridiculous. Wasn't it? She might never know. The idea saddened her. If this man knew her father—knew anything at all about him—she wanted to hear it. She and her father had always been so close. Only these past few months after his retirement had that changed. At first, she'd thought it was only because she was so busy, but now she wasn't sure. Snippets of conversations, excuses for not visiting her in California, a seeming need to get off the phone whenever she called, all came back to her now.

It had to be associated with that hidden file she'd found. Somehow her father had gotten involved with something that had consumed his last days. But what? Mr. O'Riley had assured her that he hadn't seen her father since his retirement. If her father hadn't been involved with his former colleagues, then who?

Another question she might never find an answer to.

"Time for bed," she said to John. She was exhausted. He had to be as well. Especially considering he'd been shot only a couple of days ago. She took the picture from his hand and set it aside. She hadn't mentioned the shooting or the rapid healing to Doc. Maybe she should have.

She just didn't know.

In the guest room, she pulled the covers back and gestured to the bed. "Take off your shoes and jeans, if you'd like, and cover up. Okay?"

He just stared at her as if she'd spoken in Russian or Greek. She sighed and ushered him onto the side of the bed. After dragging off his hiking boots, she stood.

"Good night." No way was she taking off his pants again. She didn't have the strength left to fight the wicked fantasies associated with the effort.

Leaving the hall light on for his benefit, she went into her own room and peeled off her clothes. When she'd pulled on a nightgown and brushed her teeth, she crawled into bed without giving in to any of her other nighttime rituals, like deep cleansing her face and applying moisturizer. Right now, she didn't give a hoot if the negligence garnered her a half dozen more wrinkles. She'd hardly slept at all last night. She had to get some sleep tonight or risk collapsing on the drive to Richmond tomorrow.

She couldn't remember being this tired since her first year as a resident. She just needed to sleep...

The mattress shifted and her eyes popped open. She sat straight up and swallowed back a scream when her gaze met John's in the darkness. The light from the hall provided just enough illumination for her to recognize his unforgettable face.

He ushered her back down onto her pillows and snuggled in close to her. Only then did she realize that he'd stripped off his jeans and T-shirt, leaving nothing between them but his thin briefs and her even thinner gown. The heavy weight of his arm over her waist as he spooned in behind her made her breath catch. But it was his softly sighed word so close to her ear that made her heart flutter like a trapped bird.

"Good," he murmured.

Chapter Seven

She lay very still, her eyes closed. He listened closely, heard her breathing. Felt the beat of her heart where his arm lay against her chest. Good.

Carefully he eased into a sitting position. The air felt cold against his skin as he moved away from her. He sat very still, watching, waiting for her eyes to open. Light came through the windows, but only a little. He blinked...wondered about that.

He no longer felt the pain. His shoulder no longer hurt, but his head remained confused. He thought of Dani...*her*. His gaze settled on the woman lying so still on the bed. Her dark hair fanned across the pillow. He remembered the deep brown of her eyes...the sound of her voice...the smell of her skin. But he couldn't remember what he was called. She called him John but instinctively he knew that was not right. She had called her friend *Doc*. Called the man in the photographs *father*...her father...Daniel Archer.

He knew Daniel Archer...somehow.

He did not know if John—if he—had a father. When

he looked in the mirror he recognized the face…light colored hair, blue eyes, but he did not know the man. Who was John? His gaze drifted to the woman once more. She wanted to know who John was as well. He was not sure he knew *her*. He only knew that some part of him felt compelled to be near her…to keep her close.

She was important to the man in the mirror.

Daniel Archer was as well.

He just couldn't remember how.

He tried to remember. But the thoughts wouldn't come.

But he was not worried. He grew stronger and learned more with the passage of time. He understood much more today than he had yesterday or even last night. He now recognized many of her feelings—fear, worry. The smooth skin of her face lined when she experienced worry. There was a catch in her breathing and her hands trembled when she felt fear, as she had last night when he came to her. She had thought to close her eyes in sleep in this room while he closed his eyes in the other, but he needed her near. Keeping her near was of the utmost importance; he sensed this with complete certainty.

Her lids fluttered open and the dark brown of her eyes showed. For one moment she lay unmoving, looking without turning her head. Then she moved. Sat up very straight and looked directly at him where he sat on the far edge of the bed near her feet. That catch in her breathing echoed in the quiet of the room and he saw her hand tremble as she brought it to her face.

This fear confused him. Was she fearful of him even now? He eased closer, studied her reaction. Her eyes widened and the fluttering at the base of her throat grew more rapid. He reached toward her and she stopped breathing entirely as his hand came to rest on her chest. He felt her heart pounding. Her fear made it beat faster. Using his fingertips, he touched the fluttering place at her throat—the pulse was also very fast. This was fear. He recognized it on a level he did not fully understand. When he withdrew his hand she sucked in a harsh breath.

"I...don't understand," he said. His voice made him flinch. How could he not remember his own voice? "You helped me to heal, but you fear me?"

She chewed on her bottom lip. He watched, thinking that she did this often. He tasted his own bottom lip but did not feel the need to do it repeatedly as she did. She watched him as well. He waited for her to answer his question.

"I helped you to heal—to get better—because I'm a doctor. That's what I do. I help people who are injured or sick."

He liked the sound of her voice. It was not harsh as his own was. Hers was soft, soothing, like the music he had heard in her car. The radio.

"I no longer have pain. You have no reason to fear me," he explained.

She smiled. "I'm glad you're feeling well." She looked at his shoulder and that worried face appeared. Lines creased the smooth skin, the shine in her eyes dulled.

"Why do you look at me that way?" he demanded. He did not like the lines on her face or the fear she felt when he was near. He had done nothing to cause the fear.

She shook her head and the lines disappeared. The smile returned and he felt better. "I'm intrigued," she told him though he wasn't sure he understood. "You healed so quickly. It's very unusual."

Unusual he understood. He didn't know why, but he understood unusual. "You feel fear when you are intrigued?" He would know the reason for her fear.

She lifted one shoulder and let it fall. "Sometimes." She touched his arm. Her fingers felt cool and soft against his skin, but something warm stirred deep inside him at her touch. He didn't understand that either.

"You're a stranger," she told him. "I don't even know your name, that makes me a little afraid—fearful," she explained.

"You call me John," he argued. "Does that not satisfy your need for a name?"

Dani couldn't help smiling again. It completely amazed her how far he'd come in so few hours. His vocabulary and ability to reason and understand increased so quickly that it boggled her mind. Yet there was still a lot he didn't understand. There had to be a way to make him comprehend her apprehension associated with his presence.

"You're a man," she went on, "I'm a woman. You're much stronger than me. I don't know you very well and that makes me a little nervous and afraid."

He stared down at himself, then at her—first her face, then her chest, specifically her scantily clad breasts. She certainly wouldn't have slept in this spaghetti-strapped negligee had she known he would be joining her. She hadn't actually brought a gown with her in her haste to get to her father. This thing had been here for ages. She'd inadvertently left it on one of her weekend visits. Now she wished she'd selected one of her father's oversized T-shirts. But she'd been too tired to go digging in boxes.

"I understand," John said abruptly.

She frowned, certain he couldn't possibly. If he only knew how his being near, wearing nothing but those boxer briefs, made her feel, he'd probably run for his life. She had been without sex, without the feel of a man's arms around her, for entirely too long. Sleeping next to him last night had made for some erotic dreams. She should be ashamed of herself, she knew, but she simply couldn't muster the necessary humility. He was beautiful and blatantly male. Even now, the lower part of his anatomy made her mouth go dry with need and she was purposely not even looking. She didn't have to look. The feel of him nestled against her backside was permanently imprinted on her memory.

He touched her forehead and she gasped. A frown worked its way across his brow in question. "This is not good."

His fingers traced the frown lines on her forehead. She reached for his other hand and touched his fingertips to his own forehead. "We do this when we don't understand something or we're concerned."

He nodded. "And this." He touched her mouth as she bit down on her lower lip and heat shot straight through her.

She swallowed to dampen her throat. He didn't understand why she bit her lip. "I do that sometimes, too, when I don't understand something."

He chewed his lip and nodded.

Silence lapsed around them for a while. He appeared content to simply look at her, but she couldn't take it for long. Those blue eyes were just too intense. "We should get ready for your appointment with the neurologist."

He stood when she did and thankfully didn't give her any trouble about shaving or taking a shower alone. She wasn't sure she could handle seeing him naked again today.

As she drove to Richmond, he seemed to absorb like a sponge everything he saw and heard. He liked the radio, particularly the music. He frowned when the news or a commercial aired. The sky and the landscape occupied a good deal of his attention, particularly when they approached the city. The tall buildings and numerous cars made him a little edgy. She suddenly worried that he might freak out and turn uncontrollable but, thankfully, he didn't.

The wait in the lobby of the neurologist's office was minimal. Dani was pleased with Dr. Nevin immediately. She approved of his bedside manner and was impressed with his methods. The way he put John at ease went a long way with making her feel more comfortable.

Now, as she and John waited, Dr. Nevin reviewed the CT scans. He'd already performed a neurological screening. She worked hard at not fidgeting in her chair. John sat on the end of the examination table, his gaze following every move the doctor made.

"There is definitely some damage." He pointed to the scan. "It's quite moderate considering the extent of his amnesia." He cocked his head and peered at the scan from a slightly different angle. "But there's something more. Take a look," he said to Dani.

She rose and stepped nearer, her gaze glued to the scan in question.

"You see this." He pointed to a spot at the very base of the skull where the spinal cord, the medulla, attached. "There's something there that shouldn't be."

She could see it, just barely. The object was tiny. "Any theories?"

"Nonmetal," he concluded. "But definitely not organic." He shook his head. "It would take an exploratory to be certain."

That was completely out of the question. Dani could not in good conscience authorize that kind of procedure without contacting John's next of kin. To do that, she had to know who he was or it had to be a medical necessity.

"Is there any chance of him regaining his memory?" She knew the answer but maybe there was new clinical evidence since she'd studied this sort of injury. A neurologist would keep up on that kind of thing more than a general practitioner.

Nevin heaved a sigh and crossed one arm over his chest so that he could brace the other on it and stroke his bearded chin. "Under normal circumstances, I would say absolutely not. Contrary to popular fiction, one doesn't generally regain any lost memories after brain damage extensive enough to produce global amnesia. Maybe a snippet or two, but nothing really. For that matter, a patient usually has to relearn to walk, to eat, everything."

Dani nodded. She'd recognized similar patterns in John.

Nevin turned his attention to the patient. "But from what you've told me, he has been on an accelerated course."

"Very much so," she assured him. "John's vocabulary increases by the minute. His fine motor skills are practically normal already. He's still learning to perceive emotion, but it's coming lightning fast."

Nevin shook his head slowly from side to side. "He definitely is not a textbook case. On the CT scan, the injury looks old, months, possibly years. But your examination revealed a lump only two days ago that, as you say, disappeared with lightning speed. It's as if the injury occurred and healed in…a matter of days."

"It sounds incredible, I know." If she'd only had Nevin's statements to go on, she'd have sworn he didn't believe her, but she could see by his posture and the expression on his face that he did, indeed, believe her.

"The gunshot wound is particularly intriguing as well." He approached John and examined the injury.

John didn't flinch or draw away. "You say it's less than a week old."

She nodded. "Startling, isn't it?"

Nevin adopted his chin-stroking stance once more. "Part of me wants to admit him and study his progress until I've appeased my raging curiosity."

Dani stiffened with a whole new kind of tension.

He sighed dramatically. "But, alas, that would not be ethical. This man has no idea who he is. His family may be searching for him. Since his condition is stable and improving, there is no reason for me to hospitalize him." He turned to Dani. "However, once his next of kin is located, I would very much like the first chance at trying to solve this mysterious riddle."

Dani managed a smile. "I'll be sure to suggest that they bring him to you."

The doctor studied her for a moment. "What steps are you taking to learn his identity?"

"I'm working with the state police," she fudged. She actually was going straight to the local office as soon as she was finished here. The doctor didn't need to know that she hadn't done that first.

"Well." He shook Dani's hand and then John's. "Good luck in your search. I'm sure John's family will greatly appreciate your efforts, Dr. Archer."

Dani settled the bill and led John back to the car. The heavy weight of sadness she felt was ridiculous, she knew, but there was no getting around it. She had a life in California to get back to and John had one as well… someplace.

She settled behind the wheel of her father's car and fastened her seat belt. John did the same. He wasn't a stray dog or an orphaned child. He was a full-grown man who belonged somewhere. To *someone,* most likely.

One way or another she had to get used to that.

THE INVESTIGATOR'S OFFICE was located in the Missing Persons Division of the Virginia State Police building. The moment they entered the facility, John tensed visibly. His apprehension was understandable since Dani felt damned apprehensive herself.

Investigator Davidson stood a full foot shorter than John and had gained himself a bulging middle from a couple of decades behind a desk. His off-the-rack suit had wrinkled from sitting at a conference table the entire morning for Friday briefings. He'd informed her of his morning agenda in the process of apologizing profusely for being tardy. His office, like the rest of the facility, was austere and uninviting. Basic government issue desks and windows draped with old-fashioned metal blinds left a lot to be desired in the way of decorating. But Investigator Davidson's pleasant smile and helpful attitude set Dani and John immediately at ease once their meeting was underway.

After Dani briefed Davidson on the situation, she and John waited while the investigator checked the system for any missing reports for Caucasian males matching John's description. He found nothing. He entered John's prints and garnered nothing there as well.

When he'd taken the necessary information and a photo to submit a complete report, he offered some advice. "Be patient." He smiled at Dani, then John. "This could take some time, but we will accomplish our goal. Someone somewhere will recognize the photo and we'll get a hit."

"Thank you, Mr. Davidson." Dani stood and offered her hand. "I'll let you know if John remembers anything useful."

John duplicated her move, extending his hand to the investigator.

Moments later, when they'd reached the car John hesitated before getting in. He looked at Dani and for the first time she saw an assurance in his eyes that was wholly out of place under the circumstances.

"He won't find anything," he said quietly.

The statement unsettled her more than she cared to admit, sent a kind of shock snapping across her nerve endings. "What makes you say that?"

John looked straight at her then; the certainty had vanished. "I don't know."

On the drive home, Dani worked hard at putting John's comment out of her mind. There was something seriously eerie about the way he'd said it. Shaking off the troubling thought, she stopped at the post office in Hickory Grove and picked up her father's mail. She hadn't bothered since she'd come home and the attendant had to retrieve the overflow from a holding area. She didn't take the time to thumb through it since John waited in the car. She didn't want to risk running into

Sheriff Nichols or any of his cronies. The last thing she needed was questions from him as to John's identity. She didn't want him involved in any way in this situation.

"Miss Dani!"

She paused at the hood of her car to look toward the voice. Cal. A smile tipped her lips. "Hey, Cal, where's your sidekick?" One rarely saw Cal without Rand or vice versa. The two were closer than brothers.

He forced a brittle smile, then stared at the ground as he shuffled his feet.

Uh-oh. This couldn't be good.

"What's wrong?" She glanced at the passenger side of her car where John waited and decided to move out of hearing range. "Talk to me, Cal," she urged as she took his arm and ushered him back toward the post office.

"It's Rand," he muttered. "He got drunk last night at the pool hall and mouthed off a little."

The hair on the back of Dani's neck stood erect. "Mouthed off about what?"

Cal sent a look toward her car. "About how he'd shot a man."

"Oh, Lord." Dani closed her eyes and scrubbed at her forehead with her free hand. She exhaled in exasperation, then fixed her gaze back on Cal. "Who did he talk to? Anyone who could cause trouble? Go to the sheriff, maybe?"

Cal shrugged. "Just a couple of the guys." He hooked his thumbs in his pockets. "I tried to smooth it over. I think it worked, but I can't be sure." Worry etched it-self across his young face. "I just felt like you ought to know. In case. I don't want Rand mad at me…but…"

She nodded. "You did the right thing, Cal." She pat-ted his arm. "I appreciate you trying to put a better spin on the situation and for keeping me informed."

"Anything new on him?" Cal angled his head to-ward the car.

"He's doing quite well. But there's no news as to who he is just yet. I've got an investigator from the state po-lice working on it. Hopefully we'll know something soon." The idea that she had scarcely more than a week before she had to be back in California broadsided her. How would she ever manage all this? She still had a few details to settle regarding her father's estate. The house had to be closed up. Final arrangements for the horses.

"I'll try to keep Rand straight," Cal promised, drag-ging her thoughts back to the here and now. "You let us know if there's anything we can do besides taking care of your horses."

She thanked Cal and climbed back into the car. John didn't ask any questions; he just studied her as she pulled out of the parking lot. He needed more clothes, she con-sidered as she drove through town. There was a super-center a few blocks away. That would do. She shifted in her seat, feeling his assessing gaze on her. He sensed her unease. But telling him the problem would be pointless.

Then again, she mused, maybe Rand needed to have to face the trouble he'd caused. Maybe protecting him was a mistake. She'd never known him to behave so foolishly. Then again, she'd behaved pretty foolishly herself. She'd taken in a complete stranger, a wounded one at that. She had no idea where he'd come from or what kind of trouble he was in. Worse yet, she'd slept in the same bed with him.

No, the worst travesty of all was that she'd wanted to do more than simply sleep next to him.

What did that make her?

A much bigger idiot than Rand could ever dream of being.

WHEN DANI had cleared away the dinner dishes and John was occupied with the evening news, she went into her father's study and picked through the mail. There were several flyers boasting sales at local department stores and supermarkets. The utility bill had to be paid, as well as the one for the telephone. Looking at the envelope from the communications company made her think about the message on the tape hidden with the file in her father's vacuum cleaner.

I think we're in trouble.

It simply didn't fit...didn't add up. Her father was an upstanding man who had never had so much as a parking ticket. How could he be involved in anything underhanded? Impossible. It was simply impossible.

She shuffled through the remaining envelopes, tossing away the ones marked current resident or box holder. Her fingers stilled as she came to a plain white business-sized envelope with no markings on the exterior other than her father's name and address and the required postmark.

Anxiety twisting in her tummy, she carefully cut the flap loose using the letter opener from her father's middle desk drawer. She reached inside the envelope and removed a single sheet of white paper, the kind used in copy machines or computer printers. The paper had been folded twice like any professionally prepared business letter. But when she opened it, there were no typewritten words, no return address, not even a salutation or closing. Five little words were scrawled in blue ink across the middle of the page.

Your execution has been ordered.

Five trauma-filled seconds passed before Dani could breathe. She read the single line again and again, and still the words jumbled one over the other in her mind. This wasn't possible…her father…

She reached for the telephone…she had to call someone.

But who?

Doc?

What would he know about this?

Nothing.

Director O'Riley?

He claimed he'd had no dealings with her father since his retirement.

Her heart racing, she snatched up the envelope again and studied it. Nothing. Plain…white. No return address. The postmark…she squinted to better make out the dim imprint…was from Alexandria. She exhaled a ragged breath. That didn't help. Alexandria lay squarely between Washington and Hickory Grove.

Anyone from either direction could have mailed the letter in Alexandria.

But why would anyone in Hickory Grove want to harm her father? He had no enemies here. She bit down on her lip. Except maybe for Lane Nichols, local sheriff and all-around jerk. But that incident had happened years ago. Why would he suddenly seek vengeance on her father?

She shook her head. That was too far-fetched. Too unlikely. Her father's death had been an accident.

She looked at the handwriting again.

Recognition flared.

"Oh, God."

Leaving the letter on her father's desk, Dani rushed to the hall closet and dragged out the Hoover. Her hands shaking, she quickly fumbled with the zipper that enclosed the collection bag and reached inside for the disk and the tape, then rushed back to her father's computer. She shoved the digital storage stick into the CPU and clicked the necessary keys to open the documents filed there. Her gaze went directly to the signed report her father had scanned into the document. *Joseph Marsh* was scrawled across the signature line. She looked from the signature to the words on the page in her hand and her heart stumbled to a halt.

It was the same.

The *s*'s, the *e*'s, the *a*'s…all exactly alike.

Joseph Marsh had worked with her father…with O'Riley.

She turned the envelope over again and checked the

date on the postmark. As her brain absorbed the ramifications of what her eyes saw, her heart thundered back into a frantic pace.

The letter had been postmarked two days before her father's *accidental* death.

Joseph Marsh had warned him that his execution had been ordered. Her father was notorious for not checking his mail on a regular basis. He'd claimed that telephones, faxes and computers had eliminated the necessity. Anyone important would use one of those means of communication.

Why hadn't Joseph Marsh?

Had he feared that the phones were tapped? The computer bugged?

Her hands started to shake.

She'd never been one to believe in conspiracy theories but…her father was dead.

I think we're in trouble.

Your execution has been ordered.

Two warnings from the same man. An old friend and colleague.

"What is it that puts fear in you, Dani?"

The sound of John's voice jerked her attention to the door.

She set the letter aside and stood. "Everything's fine." She shut down the computer and removed the storage stick, quickly placing it, as well as the letter, in the pocket of her slacks. She'd have to put both back into her father's hiding place after John had gone to bed. She forced a smile. "I'm just tired, that's all."

Ignoring his continued scrutiny, she crossed the room. When she reached the door, he didn't step aside as she'd expected. Instead, he looked at her hands, then looked her square in the eyes.

"Is it your father?"

She trembled at the idea that he could so easily read her. He shouldn't be able to do that, especially considering his own problems. "My father died. I told you that." She hadn't meant to sound curt, but her emotions were raw. Denial was roaring through her, making her chest hurt and her eyes burn with the need to cry. None of this was possible. She refused to believe her father had become involved with anyone capable of murder. It just wasn't plausible.

"Does his death make you afraid?" John persisted, those intense blue eyes searching hers.

"Yes, John," she admitted, too shaken to do otherwise. "It makes me very afraid."

"Nothing will hurt you, Dani Archer," he stated with a kind of knowing that unsettled her all the more. "No one will get past me."

Though she couldn't fathom how, Dani felt as certain of his words as she'd ever felt of anything in her life…as certain as he appeared to be.

She was safe with this stranger.

Chapter Eight

The next morning, Dani immediately noted two things about John. He seemed more quiet than usual and he'd gone outside—without her—to get the road map from her father's car. He had sat at the kitchen table studying it as if it held the secrets to his true identity and past.

She didn't like that he'd gone outside, but it wasn't as if she could have stopped him. He was head and shoulders taller than her and likely outweighed her by eighty or so pounds.

He wore the new jeans and shirt she'd purchased for him in town the day before. Thankfully, he'd also managed his shower without a reminder from her or any assistance. As grateful as she was for that reprieve, that meant she hadn't gotten a look at his shoulder. Judging by his past progress she imagined that it was completely healed by now. She needed to go online and do some research on speed healers. She remembered reading about the phenomenon back in med school.

Now, as the sunlight waned in the west, she braced her hands on the counter and stared out the kitchen window. Morning had come and gone, as had the afternoon, with her making the final calls necessary to settle her father's estate. She had sealed up the last of the boxes containing his things.

John had surveyed her home, looking at photo albums and framed photographs as if they would teach him something about his own past. He'd questioned her about her life, as well as her father's, and then spent hours seemingly contemplating the knowledge she had shared.

But it didn't matter how she attempted to occupy herself—the letter kept intruding on her thoughts.

Could her father have been murdered?

She winced at the idea. One of Sheriff Nichols' deputies had investigated the scene and proclaimed it an accident. Doc had assisted with the autopsy himself. He'd assured Dani that her father's injuries were consistent with a fall from the roof of the barn.

But was that fall an accident? Could he have been pushed? She shook her head, a troubled sigh seeping past her lips. That just couldn't be. Her father had never harmed anyone in his life. Why would anyone want to harm him? He had always preached morals and ethics. It seemed impossible that he would fall short of his own proudly held and widely proclaimed standards and gotten involved with unsavory characters.

"This is where we are."

Dani turned at the sound of John's voice. He had resumed his map quest once more. As she followed his gaze, he pointed to the map spread on the table and then looked up at her questioningly. A frown annoyed her brow as she walked over to look at the map. Why was he so concerned with their location? He didn't even know his name. What difference did anything else make? Dani forced herself to breathe. Two deep breaths. This wasn't John's fault. She couldn't take her misery out on him. This was not about him.

She peered at the map for a time, then nodded. "Yes." She touched the place he'd marked with pencil. "The ranch is here. Hickory Grove there." The small town had managed, unbelievably, to get on the map. "We drove to Richmond yesterday morning." She tapped a spot south of Hickory Grove.

His head bent studiously, John considered the area without asking any other questions. Maybe she wasn't the only one who needed a distraction. From the corner of her eye, Dani glimpsed a vehicle approaching the house. She moved back to the window and took a closer look.

Panic struck like a runaway bull charging a too cocky matador.

A county vehicle. The markings identified the SUV as belonging to the sheriff's department.

She moistened her lips and tamped down the hysteria crowding into her throat. She had to be calm here. If it was *him,* it wasn't as if she hadn't come face-to-face with him in all these years. He'd attended her father's funeral. Had even offered his seemingly sincere condolences. She'd just been too overwhelmed to notice or care.

But this was different.

There could only be one of two explanations for why he was here now. Either he'd heard Rand's story from someone who'd been at the pool hall last night or Investigator Davidson had ratted her out.

Neither scenario appealed to her.

Still, this was her ranch, her responsibility. She had no choice but to face the problem head-on.

"Do you know that man?"

John's deep voice gave her a start. She looked up to find him next to her, peering out the window above the kitchen sink. Lane Nichols climbed from the vehicle and surveyed her yard. Whether by design or happenstance, he chose that precise moment to adjust the weapon at his side.

She took a deep, bolstering breath. "Yes. He's the sheriff in this county. I'll need to go outside and see what he wants." She moistened her lips and balled her fists in preparation for battle. "I want you to stay in here, John. Don't come outside. I don't want him asking any more questions than necessary. I don't trust him."

Dani couldn't be sure if John actually understood, but he nodded all the same.

She left him in the kitchen, choosing to exit the house from the front door. If the sheriff insisted on coming inside, the entry hall was as far as she intended to invite him. A shudder of dread twisted through her. She did not want to be within ten miles of him, much less face-to-face with the bastard. But she had no choice. She couldn't just ignore him. Unfortunately, he wouldn't go away.

By the time she'd reached the door, he'd crossed the porch and knocked once. She smoothed her hands over her jeans to wipe away the dampness and braced herself for battle. She opened the door and stepped out onto the porch, forcing him to make room.

"What do you want, Nichols?" She refused to use his title. As far as she was concerned, he didn't deserve that much respect.

He tipped his hat and grinned from ear to ear. "Why, Dani, that's no way to say hello," he tossed back in what he no doubt considered a jovial, if not charming, tone.

"Unless you have official business here," she replied, "I'd like you off my property." How was that for hello? she mused.

Lane Nichols could be called nothing less than attractive if one were to consider his physical assets only. He was tall, well built, had thick brown hair, the naturally highlighted, summer-blond kind, and sparking hazel eyes. There wasn't a single thing unattractive about the thirty-something man, except his black heart.

As quick as a wink, his disposition changed. The ugly side of him that she'd experienced up close and personal once too often already lashed out at her. "I'll go when I'm ready," he said quietly, so damned quietly she shuddered. As quiet as his voice had been, she hadn't missed the ferocity of it. He was madder than hell at her audacity. As county sheriff, he was accustomed to a certain level of cooperation.

"What do you want?" she repeated her earlier demand. She wished she had thought to bring the cordless phone receiver outside with her. The one on the hall table…just a mere dozen feet away. The one she'd had to pass to answer the door. Then she could have called 911 if he became too aggressive. Too late now.

"I want to know what happened on that mountain of yours with Randall Williams and Calvin Peacock." He gestured toward the area where Rand and Cal hunted. He leaned in closer and sneered at her. "And don't even think about lying to me, *Dr. Archer*. I've already heard one version of it today."

Dani took stock of the situation, mostly to buy time. Nichols stood squarely between her and her father's car—not that she had the keys on her, but she could lock herself inside if need be. He wore his sidearm at his waist in plain view, his right hand stationed right next to it in an intimidating manner. He wanted her scared. Unfortunately, she didn't let him down on that score.

"Don't believe everything you hear, *Sheriff*." She mocked his tone in spite of her fear. "Rand is a kid, so is Cal. If what you heard came out of one of the beer bashes at the pool hall, then I wouldn't put much stock in any of it if I were you."

He stabbed her in the chest with his forefinger. She winced and resisted the urge to move back a step. "But you're not me," he blustered angrily. "Now start talking."

"The boys hunt on my property," she shot back with just as much fury. "My father gave them permission. I can't say what they do when they get up there on that mountain." She lifted her chin and stared into those cruel eyes. "I doubt you can, either, unless, of course, you're psychic."

Big mistake.

He manacled her arms before she could escape his reach and slammed her against the side of the house, not two feet from the door she'd hoped to flee through. Her heart rammed mercilessly against her rib cage as flashes of memory whizzed past her mind's eye. Him forcing her down onto the ground. Her clothes ripping from her body…his suffocating weight…

"Listen, bitch," he growled, "I want to know if the story about Rand shooting a man is true. If it is, then I'm going to haul your pretty little ass in for aiding and abetting. Now. Did Rand shoot someone?"

"Let me go, you bastard." She hurled the words at him with all the bravado she possessed. As frightened as she was, she would be damned if she'd let him see the extent. She wouldn't give him the perverse pleasure.

A sick smile slid across his face. Too late. He knew exactly how terrified she was. "Maybe I'll just teach you that lesson you missed out on all those years ago." He ground his hips into hers, making her stomach churn with disgust. She shoved hard at him, her entire body seizing in revulsion.

"I said let me go!"

"I don't think so," he growled savagely, his mouth so close to hers she could feel his hot breath on her skin.

"Let her go."

Nichols jerked his head up but didn't release her. Her heart jarred to a near halt when her gaze landed on John standing in the open doorway.

"Who the hell are you?" Nichols demanded. His fingers dug painfully into her arms. Dani winced, but bit back the cry that burgeoned in her throat.

"Let her go," John repeated.

A new kind of fear seared through Dani as she stared at the man who would be her savior. There was something about his eyes. A savage intensity beyond anything she'd ever seen before. Barbaric…almost inhuman. She blinked and looked again. He stood perfectly still yet motion…energy seemed to hum around him. His entire demeanor looked deadly…he looked poised to kill.

Nichols shoved her aside and went toe-to-toe with John. "I asked you a question," he snarled. "Who the hell are you?"

A lethal smile slid across John's lips. "The last man you'll ever look in the eye if you aren't careful," he said softly, too damned softly.

For a second that turned into five, Dani was sure Nichols intended to back off, but then he got his second wind.

"I guess I'll just have to haul your sorry ass in," he threatened in that cocky tone that made her want to vomit.

Dani opened her mouth to argue but it was too late. One moment, Nichols stood on the porch glaring at John; the next, he was on the ground at the bottom of the steps with John on top of him.

She rushed toward them. If Nichols pulled his gun...

John's gaze collided with hers and she stopped dead in her tracks when faced with the sheer ruthlessness of it. "Stay back," he growled, the sound rumbling from deep inside his chest.

They rolled once, twice. Nichols reached for his weapon and Dani's breath stalled in her lungs. In a move like none she had ever seen before, John snatched the weapon first. Pulled it free of its sheath. Her hands went to her mouth. Dear God, don't let him...

He tossed the weapon aside just as Nichols slammed a fist into his left cheek. They rolled a couple more times before John took complete charge of the situation. Dani stood paralyzed, unable to comprehend how he could execute such precision moves. He was obviously trained to fight...knew exactly what he was doing. Nichols didn't stand a chance. Fear for the sheriff's life abruptly washed over Dani. What if John killed him?

"You broke my fingers!" Nichols yelled as John abruptly stopped and moved off him as if Dani had somehow telegraphed her concerns to him. Nichols cradled his right hand as he staggered to his feet.

A gust of bravado propelling her, Dani rushed off the porch and straight up to Nichols. "I asked you to leave," she said as firmly as she could. "Now go."

John had picked up the weapon and unloaded it, tossing the rounds into the grass. He pitched the weapon toward the sheriff's SUV, then kicked the hat Nichols had lost in the fray in that direction as well.

"Don't come back," he warned, that same ferocity in his eyes…his expression.

Dani swallowed with difficulty. Who was this man?

"I won't forget this," Nichols snarled. He looked from John to Dani. "Count on it."

He grabbed his hat and the now impotent weapon with his good hand as he stumbled toward his vehicle. Not until he'd roared down the drive leaving behind a cloud of dust did Dani dare let go the breath she'd been holding.

John stood there staring at her in the weak light; his expression had relaxed back into the guileless, expectant one she'd come to associate with him. His eyes had lost their savage glower. He looked suddenly weary and only then did she notice his bleeding lip and swelling cheek.

"He hurt you." She rushed over to him and took a better look. She reached up to touch his cheek and winced.

"Did he hurt you?"

Some of the ferocity was back. He looked ready and fully capable of killing. For the first time since he'd stumbled into her home, Dani felt a full measure of true fear…terror, actually. This man was dangerous. She thought of the way he'd fought; Nichols had no idea how close he'd come to losing his life. Of that she was certain. And only two days ago, this man, John, had seemingly been on the verge of death. He'd suffered serious brain trauma, been shot, and still he fought like a…like a wild animal—desperately and without conscience or remorse of any sort.

"I'm fine," she insisted when she found her voice. "He didn't hurt me, just shook me up a little."

John surveyed her as if making his own assessment. "You're certain?"

It was so hard for her to believe that he'd scarcely been able to utter a solitary word less than forty-eight hours ago. "Yes. Please, let's go inside," she urged, taking his arm and ushering him toward the house. "You're the one who's injured."

Dani closed and locked the door, the whole time praying that Nichols wouldn't come back with a whole posse of his cohorts. There was no telling what he would do…or attempt to do to John if he came back. Rand. Dammit. Why hadn't he kept his mouth shut? He would get a stern talking-to for this. She'd helped him out and this was the repayment she received. Some friend.

John moved up the stairs more slowly than usual. She watched him, noting stiffness rather than the fluid motion she'd observed in him recently. Was he hurt worse than she knew? Maybe the exertion was simply too much for him. After all, she had no way of knowing how long he'd been wandering injured in the woods. He was likely out of shape. She sighed as she led him the final few steps to the bathroom adjoining her bedroom. He darn sure didn't look out of shape, but she knew looks could be deceiving.

She ushered him down onto the closed toilet lid and surveyed his injuries. She needed an ice pack for the cheek, but the lip required a thorough cleaning and antibiotic ointment.

"Take off your shirt," she ordered. She might as well get a look at that shoulder while she was at it.

He obeyed without hesitation. She almost laughed out loud. It just felt so damned ironic to have watched this guy tear the sheriff apart and then obey her slightest command as if she held some power over him.

Every woman's fantasy, she ruminated.

Her gaze fell upon his shoulder and the sight took her aback. She reached out, touched the unmarred flesh. How the hell? There wasn't even a scar. That wasn't possible...

"It's better, yes?"

She turned to those questioning eyes. How could he look so innocent, so utterly guileless, after what she'd witnessed only minutes ago in her front yard?

"Yes," she answered. "It's better."

She forced her attention back to the task at hand by wetting a clean washcloth and using it to wipe away the blood from his chin and cheek. His skin felt warm and smooth. She tried not to allow her gaze to roam over his chest but she couldn't help herself. He was so beautifully made.

Chastising herself for being an idiot, she applied an antiseptic cleanser to the busted lip. He didn't even wince, just watched her with that single-minded intensity that somehow peeled away her every defense.

"I should get you an ice pack." She took a breath, tried to smile, but a frown tugged her lips downward. She'd forgotten the antibiotic cream. But then, with his rapid healing why bother?

That handsome face rearranged into a frown of his own. "Why are your hands shaking? Are you still afraid?"

Good grief. How did she explain? She dragged in another much needed breath. "No. No, I'm not afraid."

"But your respiration is irregular and you are trembling," he countered, his gaze never leaving hers.

She rubbed at the back of her neck, noting somewhere in the far reaches of her brain that the bun she'd tucked her hair into this morning was now hanging more around her neck than on her head. Irregular respiration? Had he heard Doc use that phrase? How would John know to put her current state in those terms? "Really," she insisted. "I'm not afraid."

He took her hands in his and held them gently. "I won't allow him to hurt you. There is no need to show fear."

Why didn't he just let it go? She moistened her lips and managed another smile. "It's not fear, John," she said pointedly as she tried to pull her hands away. Now who wasn't letting the subject go? Why didn't she allow him to believe what he would? Stupid. So stupid.

He stood, forcing her to take a step away, but he didn't release her hands. "Explain this reaction, if it is not fear," he insisted.

Oh, yes. Way stupid. She'd literally backed herself into a corner. What the hell? "It's a man-woman thing, John," she said, boiling it down to its most basic form. Why pretend? "You're…" She allowed her gaze to roam over his chest, to trace the shadows and angles of that awesome face. "I'm attracted to you physically. I don't mean to be," she added hastily. "But I can't help it. It's chemistry."

His scowl of confusion deepened. "I don't understand."

She nodded. "I know you don't and I'm sorry. I'm just an idiot, okay?" The blush started at her toes and raced all the way to the roots of her hair. Did a more lame excuse for her behavior even exist?

Not likely.

"Make me understand."

The softly spoken words were more of a command than a statement. The intensity of that gaze on hers was very nearly more than she could bear. This close, the sensual pull was overpowering.

"John, I'm not sure that's a good idea." Every fiber of her being—every part of her that made her a woman—cried out for her to show him exactly what she meant.

"We'll see," he whispered.

The two words were scarcely a shadow of sound but more emotionally moving than any she'd ever heard. Saying no was not an option.

Bracing her hands against that muscular chest, she tiptoed, pressed her lips to his and kissed him tenderly. A shock sizzled through her, sending all her senses on alert. The texture of his skin was as smooth as glass beneath her palms, incredibly so, like silk encasing steel.

He didn't move, held perfectly still, his hands still wrapped loosely around her forearms.

Floating on a cloud of pure sensation, Dani drew back from that full, firm mouth and stared up at him. She felt warm and tingly inside. "That's what I've been longing to do every time I look at you." She sighed a dreamy sound and suddenly she didn't care how lame her actions were. She'd needed desperately to do that. It was done. Get over it, she ordered, but her traitorous body refused to listen.

As if his own lust had abruptly kicked in, his fingers tightened around her arms and he dragged her to him, bringing his mouth down on hers with such force that she tasted the tang of blood mixed with antiseptic from his injured lip. He kissed her harder than she'd ever been kissed before. Her arms went up around his neck and she leaned into the kiss, letting him have his way with her. It was almost too forceful and urgent to be pleasant, but the fire he'd started deep inside her wouldn't let her slow him down. She wanted this...wanted it desperately.

When at last he came up for air, she tugged him into the bedroom. His eyes were glazed with desire and he looked desperate to make some move, but wasn't sure how to proceed. The idea of teaching him fueled her own desire. She drew his hands to her breasts and squeezed them around her. Need shot straight to her feminine core. Her eyes closed and she moaned with the sweetness of it.

John proved a quick study. He tore away her blouse and bra to gain better access. He squeezed and kneaded her breasts until her knees were weak. She wanted to get naked and into the bed. With him! Now!

She helped him out of his jeans and briefs, tossing shoes and socks aside as she went. He gave her the same treatment, only more slowly. Since he'd never seen her naked, he took his time, learning every square inch he revealed before moving on. By the time her jeans and panties landed on the floor, she was ready to scream with climax.

She eased back onto the bed, drawing him onto the cool sheets with her. He stretched out beside her and looked at her as if he couldn't get enough of simply looking. His fully aroused sex nudged her belly and her entire body quivered with need and the knowledge that every part of him was so very wonderfully made.

"Touch me," she whispered, her voice shaking with the need already way out of control inside her.

He obeyed, trailing his fingers over her skin as if she were as fragile as delicate glass and considerably more precious. Heat followed his path like red-hot licking flames. Her body began to undulate and writhe of its own accord. She edged closer to release. She closed her eyes and reveled in the sensual pleasure of the incredible journey. It had been so very long. She wouldn't let herself think about right or wrong…about consequences or tomorrow.

His mouth closed over her nipple and she cried out at the new explosion of sensations. He hesitated, uncertain.

"Please," she urged. "Don't stop."

As he suckled, she dragged his hand down to the damp curls between her thighs. She was already plenty wet…plenty ready, but, selfishly, she wanted more.

He delved into her drenched folds, prodded the sensitive flesh before two powerful fingers slipped deeply inside her. Her muscles convulsed around him, sending spiral after spiral of exquisite pleasure coursing through her. He slid those strong fingers back and forth, probing her velvet depths with avid curiosity, drawing her fierce concentration to that central point. Climax came hard and fast. She gasped, cried out his name and bucked against his hand. He watched in awe, his lips parted, his breath coming as hard and fast as her throbbing orgasm.

She took a moment to catch her breath and enjoy the afterglow. He watched, trailed those damp fingers along her skin, sending tingle after tingle over her aroused flesh. Unable to resist another second, she pushed him onto his back. He went down willingly, the sight of his erect sex sending tremors through her body. She straddled him and placed his hands on her hips. The anticipation lighting those blue eyes was enough to push her to the very edge all over again, but she wanted more. She wanted *him* inside *her*.

Like she told him, it was a man-woman thing.

She positioned him at her entrance. His eyes closed and he made a savage sound deep in his throat. She wanted this to be something he would not forget. If he never regained his memory, this would be his first time. She wanted it to be special.

Her hips pressed downward, taking him inside only an inch or two. His fingers dug into her flesh but he fought the urge he no doubt felt to drag her downward, burying himself completely. She saw the fine tremor in his arms as he battled the surely irresistible need, or maybe he didn't know what to do. The thought thrilled her. She pressed down another inch, her own body fighting her now, wanting more when it was already stretched to capacity by his thick sex. She licked her lips and moved upward just an inch, maybe two. He roared his disapproval, clasped her hips tighter. A fine sheen of sweat glistened on his skin and she couldn't resist leaning down to brush her lips against his.

Her feminine walls throbbed with need, urging her to take all of him inside her, but still she resisted, wanting to make it last, needing to drive him crazy.

He kissed her back as she moved her hips up and down, just an inch or two in either direction, slow, deliberate pulses. Up. Down. Slowly. The tension mounted. Sweat slickened her skin as she struggled with the need to take him fully. She kept it slow. Up. Down.

And then he moved.

Took charge.

One hand fisted in her hair while the other cupped her bottom. He had her under him in a single flourish of movement. His gaze locked with hers and he thrust fully, deeply inside her. Her second orgasm burst forth, sending hot shivers across every nerve ending as he filled her so completely that she felt certain she would not survive the supreme pleasure.

He pumped hard and deep. She gasped for air… clutched at his massive chest as, incredibly, the tension started to build inside her all over again. How was that possible? She'd already come twice. She groaned, couldn't catch her breath. Suddenly he stopped. He looked deep into her eyes and growled one word.

"Good."

She gasped, her heart thudding dangerously in her chest. His hips flexed, drawing him back to the tip before he drove into her. Harder. Deeper. Faster. Until she came apart all over again, shattering into shards of quivering ecstasy. For that one moment in time everything stopped, even her heart. In that infinitesimal instant of minideath he took that helpless organ from her without even trying, without even knowing his own name. And then release exploded through him, taking him to that same place where she'd already been…three times.

He stilled, his breath coming in ragged bursts, and stared into her eyes, their bodies as one. He was right. It was so very *good*. And suddenly it didn't matter if she ever knew his name.

Chapter Nine

"Director."

O'Riley knew someone was calling him but he wasn't ready to leave the dream. His wife…Angela… was there. She'd changed her mind about leaving him. He would take her back…forgive her. Nothing else mattered as long as they were reunited. He missed her so much…

"Director!"

O'Riley jerked awake and straightened. He blinked twice to clear his gaze. He'd fallen asleep at his desk. His face no doubt bore the marks of having slept on his hands. He clenched and unclenched his fingers to get the blood circulating again and to dispel the tingling sensation.

"What?" he snapped at Dupree. The man hovered over him like a frigging buzzard. O'Riley glanced at the clock on his desk—1:00 a.m.—then looked the intelligence analyst up and down. It irritated the hell out of him that Dupree could look so neat and polished at this hour. He'd obviously showered and shaved and changed into a fresh suit. Bastard. It wasn't right to O'Riley's way of thinking for a guy to look sharper than his boss. His own attire carried two days' wrinkles. His white shirt, once crisply starched, had wilted about thirty-six hours ago.

Dupree grinned like an idiot. "We've got him, sir."

O'Riley perked up. "Explain. Now." He had no patience for Dupree's beating around the bush.

"Late yesterday afternoon, Adam's prints were entered into the FBI's system for identification by an investigator at the Virginia State Police Department."

"You're kidding." O'Riley closed the top button on his shirt and straightened his tie. Talk about a lucky break. "Where is he? What's his condition?"

Dupree laughed nervously, then cleared his throat. "That's the strangest part of all. He's with Danielle Archer."

O'Riley's jubilant expression dropped. "I want details."

Dupree shuffled through the written notes in his hand. "Our team leader questioned Investigator Scott Davidson in his home at a little past midnight. Davidson said that Danielle Archer had brought a man she referred to as a John Doe to his office to see if there was a missing persons report matching his description."

O'Riley's brow furrowed deeply enough to give him a headache. "John Doe?"

Dupree shrugged. "Davidson said that he got the impression our man had amnesia or something along those lines."

O'Riley swore long and hotly. "What's Medical saying about this?"

A long sigh accompanied another shrug from Dupree. "Medical says it's possible, especially if there was enough trauma involved to damage the tracking device."

"What's the prognosis?" O'Riley's guts had tied into knots. Adam was their top Enforcer. The best. Losing him would be a tremendous blow to the project.

"The injury may heal itself. There's no way to know until a thorough examination is conducted. Long-term memories will more likely be preserved by his *super* gene encoding than short-term." Dupree stared at the floor, his fingers fisted around his notes.

"What?" O'Riley knew there was more.

Reluctantly Dupree met his gaze. "There's a chance that he may regain portions of his memory out of sequence which could prove to be a serious security risk. Medical is recommending—"

"Get out," O'Riley roared. He had to think this through. Had to have a moment alone. He didn't give a damn what Medical recommended.

Dupree didn't argue. He knew it was pointless. Closing the door behind him, he gave O'Riley the privacy he needed.

Adam.

He'd watched Adam mature into a man. Had applauded his unparalleled advancements. None of the others were as good as Adam. Archer had insisted that Adam's genetic enhancements had evolved perfectly.

That degree of perfection only happened on rare occasions. Adam was special.

O'Riley didn't want to lose him. There had to be a way to salvage him. He was a speed healer. Who else would have survived the kind of blunt trauma required to damage a near indestructible device like the state-of-the-art trackers Center utilized?

He refused to admit defeat.

There had to be a way.

He flipped open his secure cell phone and put a call through directly to the team leader in Virginia. He wasn't taking any chances on miscommunication.

"O'Riley here," he barked. "I have additional instructions for you." He waited while the man briefed him as to the current situation. They had reached Hickory Grove and were headed to the Archer ranch. "Good. I want you to bring Adam back to Center alive. Do you understand? Alive." The team leader assured him that he copied. "He is not to be harmed in any way." O'Riley considered the team leader's question as to what they were to do with the woman. He'd known Dani Archer since she was a child. But that didn't change the undeniable. There was no room for error…no margin for risk when it came to security. He swallowed hard and exhaled a heavy breath. "She represents a Level II security risk. Eliminate her."

JOHN WOKE abruptly.

He didn't move…listened.

Dani slept in his arms, her breathing soft and even.

But that wasn't what had awakened him.

Danger was close at hand.

Adrenaline had already started to flow, burning through his veins in warning.

They had to go.

Hurry.

An instinct he couldn't fully comprehend urged him like a voice inside his head. *Hurry.*

He eased soundlessly from the bed and tugged on his jeans and shoes. He dragged the T-shirt over his head all the while listening for the slightest sound. His senses reaching…reaching…discerning the subtle changes in the very air. He sensed the presence of others…smelled their skin…the clothes they wore…the weapons they carried. Heard the frosted grass bend beneath their boots…heard their breathing.

They were close.

His vision suddenly sharpened, cutting through the darkness.

He moved to Dani's side of the bed and crouched down close to her. "We have to leave," he murmured.

Her eyes fluttered open. "Hmmm?"

"We have to go. Now," he pressed. He drew the cover back, saw her shiver from the night air. "Hurry," he urged.

Confusion marring her expression, she reached for her jeans and slid them on. She stood then stepped into her shoes. "Where are we going?"

He touched his finger to her lips and shook his head, hoping she would understand he needed her to be very quiet. She moved toward the closet and pulled out a blouse, then wiggled into it. He remembered then that he had torn the blouse she'd been wearing in his efforts to remove it. His body tightened and his respiration escalated instantly at the memory of their joining. No time to dwell on that now.

He took her hand and moved toward the door.

A creak of the wood floor downstairs told him that they were already inside the house. He listened, closing his eyes to block visual stimuli. With visual blocked his auditory detection increased twofold. Three men. Weapons in gloved hands. Their ability to move about in the darkness without encountering obstacles indicated they wore night vision goggles.

Careful not to make a sound, he led Dani into the hall outside her room. He moved toward the small closet near the landing where the stairs met the second story. The door opened without a sound. He pushed her inside the closet, then backed in to wait, leaving the door cracked just enough to see his enemy pass their position.

The first man moved quickly past. Another came seconds later. John had his arm around his throat in two seconds. The man was dead and sprawled on the floor in less than five. John eased back into the closet to wait for the first man to come out of the bedroom he'd entered ten seconds earlier.

When he moved to his fallen comrade's side, John struck again, this time with a precise blow to that most vulnerable spot of the throat as the man looked up.

With those two down, he tugged Dani from the closet. To her credit, she had her hand over her mouth before her gasp could escape. Careful of the two treads he'd noticed that creaked, he led her downstairs. The third man would still be down here somewhere. They had assumed he and Dani were in bed and had sent two men rather than one to the most likely area where they would encounter resistance.

Others would be waiting outside.

The third man exited Dani's father's study to find John waiting for him. He went down as quickly and easily as the others.

This time, Dani wasn't quite so successful in covering her shock. John didn't give her time to question what he'd done. He dragged her through the house as quietly as he could. When this advance team failed to communicate with the other party waiting, others would come.

They had to be gone before that happened.

Once through the back door, John flattened against the back of the house, Dani followed suit. He closed his eyes and listened, inhaled deeply of the cool night air. The barn was still clear. The others were watching the front of the house. He sensed one somewhere on the back of the property, but the direction of the wind kept him from pinpointing his exact location.

He'd have to risk running into him. With Dani's hand firmly grasped in his, they started for the barn. On the far side of the barn, the pasture would provide little in the way of camouflage, but if they could make it to the edge of the woods they would be safe. John had studied the map. He knew the area.

Dani's lungs burned. Her legs ached with the effort of keeping up with John's long strides. Someone was behind them. She could hear the pounding of their steps against the grass-covered ground. One or two…she couldn't be sure. She didn't dare look back for fear of stumbling. It wasn't as if she could see anything. It was so dark and the men were dressed in black.

Ski masks, boots, guns…what did they want?

Why were they chasing her?

Your execution has been ordered.

Jeez, this couldn't be about her father.

I think we're in trouble.

For a split second, she wanted to stop, to turn around and scream at them that her father was dead. What else did they want? She knew nothing of what he'd been involved in! She shook her head at her own mental slip. Her father hadn't been involved with any wrongdoing. There had to be a mistake. If someone had killed him, it was a mistake.

Joseph Marsh.

She had to find him. He had been the one to warn her father. He would have the answers she needed.

She plunged forward against the wind, John pulling her behind him. When they reached safety, she would find a way to track down Joseph Marsh. He was the key.

What did he look like? Dani concentrated as hard as she could to remember. She was sure she'd met him at her father's retirement party. Practically everyone he'd ever worked with had been there. Marsh had to have been there, too.

She had to think.

The woods.

Thank God.

They'd reached the edge of the woods.

Something pinged against a tree to her right.

Dear God! They were being shot at!

John jerked her against him. Darted off to his left, barreling at full speed through the dense undergrowth. Limbs slapped at her legs, tore at her arms like reaching fingers. John didn't slow down for anything.

She wasn't sure how he could see in the darkness. She couldn't see anything. Somehow he avoided the trees, wove through them as if darting around an obstacle course.

Long minutes passed…or maybe hours. She couldn't be sure. She only knew that she was exhausted. So tired. The terrain inclined steadily and it was all she could do to pull oxygen into her lungs. Endorphins had kicked in, saving her from the pain she knew she should be feeling. But when that rush wore off…

She couldn't think about that right now…had to keep moving. Higher…faster. She stumbled. John caught her, steadied her back on her feet. She had to concentrate. Focus. Climb faster. Grab on to anything that would keep her moving forward.

The people chasing them had to believe she knew something about whatever had gotten her father killed. Why else would they come after her? If they caught her, she would never figure out what really happened. Never be able to bring to justice whoever had harmed her father. It all felt so surreal. Murder. Impossible. Her father had been a good, quiet man who had never harmed a soul. He loved life…loved his country. How could this happen?

Your execution has been ordered.

She had no explanation. No reason she could point to.

But somehow it had happened.

A new kind of determination burned through her. By God, they would not get away with it.

More shots whizzed past, hitting the ground or a tree. John zigzagged, dragging her along behind him.

He stopped abruptly.

She slammed into his back.

The sound of the air heaving violently in and out of her lungs startled her in the sudden quiet.

"We have to jump," he murmured roughly.

Her eyebrows pushed together in confusion. "What?"

He pulled her closer to him and pointed to something. "Jump. There."

Her heart rocketed into her throat. Her eyes rounded in absolute terror. They stood on a cliff overlooking a ravine. She couldn't make out much, except that the drop appeared to go on and on. She heard water rushing far below. The river.

"We can't!" In two seconds flat, her mind inventoried the number of bones that would likely be crushed and the internal organs that would be damaged on impact if they missed the water, perhaps even if they didn't.

"Now!" He went over the edge, taking her with him.

In the movies, when people jumped over a cliff, it always seemed to take forever for them to hit whatever was below them, water generally. But that didn't happen in this instance. They struck something hard almost immediately. The impact knocked the breath out of Dani's lungs.

Before she could gather her wits he was dragging her backward. Over another ledge? The idea seared through her brain. She struggled against him, but he was far too strong for her to break free.

Whatever light from the moon and the stars the night had offered was suddenly gone. She clapped a hand over her mouth to prevent a cry of hysteria. What the hell was he doing? Where were they?

Reason intruded in the nick of time, saving her from the tears cresting on her lashes.

Dank...dark.

A cave.

They'd hit a ledge sticking out from the side of the mountain and now he was dragging her backward into a cave.

A bat cave, most likely.

As if to prove her theory, the flapping of hundreds of tiny wings filled the air for several seconds before the cave occupants who hadn't gone out hunting settled down again.

Rabies.

Bats carried rabies.

Bats excreted all over their caves.

Her stomach roiled in protest.

As if he'd read her mind, John leaned against the wall and pulled her into his lap. He pressed his mouth to her ear and whispered, "Don't move…don't make a sound."

The warmth of his breath on her skin sent a rush of heat through her, made her feel safe. She nodded her understanding and relaxed against his chest.

He cocked his head as if listening to the night. Though she couldn't see him, she felt the movement. She remembered suspecting that his sense of hearing was well above normal. Maybe he would hear their pursuers on the cliff above them. Dani could imagine the men concluding that they had jumped into the river.

She pressed closer to John. Thank God for him. If he hadn't been there, she would be dead now.

Just like her father.

Murdered.

She closed her eyes.

Didn't want to think about it anymore.

Instead, she relived making love with John. Those moments before he understood what to do…and then those sexually explosive minutes after he'd taken charge. He'd made love to her so thoroughly that she'd been sure she would simply die of pleasure.

And then they'd showered together. This time, he'd smoothed the soap over her bare skin rather than on her wet clothes. They'd made love again in the shower. More slowly that time, more tenderly.

Anything John had forgotten about sex had come back to him completely by then. She inhaled the scent of wildflower shampoo that lingered in his hair…on his skin. She smelled of the same. A smile inched across her lips when she thought of the way his skin tasted. Smooth and smoky…just a tad salty. Very male.

Every inch of him was perfect in form and function. With the way his body healed itself, she wondered if his mind would as well. Catastrophic damage such as what he'd endured generally left massive brain damage. Was his body healing that damage even now?

Would he remember his past soon? Was there a wife or lover…a fiancée, maybe? Children? Sadness tugged at her heart. How selfish of her to want to keep him just the way he was. He deserved to know who he was and where he'd come from. If he had family and friends, he should be able to return to them. She had a life, such as it was. Was it fair for her to wish his away?

Of course not.

She wanted John to remember. She wanted him to know everything. She just prayed that in remembering the past, he wouldn't forget the present. Because right now was all they had and she didn't want to let it go.

HE ANSWERED the call on the first ring. There was no point in putting off the inevitable. He'd run from it for more than forty-eight hours.

There was no escaping.

"Yes."

"Tell me you've found it."

He cleared his throat and wished for a miracle. But he'd never been one of the lucky ones. Miracles never came along for him. He'd always had to make his own luck.

"I didn't find it."

Silence.

"You understand what this means?"

He nodded to himself, then said to the other man, "Yes, I understand."

"You're sure it's not in the house."

"Positive. I've been over every damned square foot of the place. It isn't there."

"Neither is she."

He straightened, uncertain if he wanted to know what that meant. "What do you mean, she isn't there?"

"She's on the run. They sent an Enforcer in to execute her, but something went wrong. Center sent in a retrieval team before our people could get there. Now they're both on the run. Apparently, the Enforcer has been missing for several days. Center had no idea he'd made it to his target until an investigator named Davidson from VSP ran his prints through the system."

"Why…" He cleared his throat. "Why didn't he kill her?"

"The Enforcer was damaged somehow, doesn't even remember who he is. He's protecting her now." He laughed sardonically. "Damned fool. She has no idea that the man saving her ass is the same one who was sent to kill her."

Startled by the news, he asked hesitantly, "What do you want me to do?" If he didn't find the file they would both be dead soon. It might be too late now. He had to try…anything.

"With her on the run, she's going to get desperate. She surely knows that something is wrong. She may even suspect that her father was murdered. She'll contact someone she can trust. Wait for that to happen, then do what you have to. There's always the chance she has the file with her. Find out. Then kill her."

He hung up the phone without bothering to acknowledge the orders. It wasn't necessary. He would do whatever was required of him. He would do anything to stay alive.

He only wished that it hadn't come to this.

Murder was such an ugly matter.

Chapter Ten

"How do we get out of here?" Dani peered toward the cliff far overhead. A good twenty feet straight up with nothing more than the occasional protruding rock or root to grasp and even those were few and far between. Looking down then, she estimated that the drop to the water was at least sixty or seventy feet. God only knew if the water was deep enough to compensate for the kind of momentum the plunge would generate.

"We go down," John said, calculating the distance with his eyes as she had just done. "If we fall, at least the water will be beneath us."

Yeah, right.

Dani peeked over the ledge and swallowed hard. The ledge protruded a mere four feet. The fact that they'd landed on it in the dark last night was a miracle. Her gaze shifted to the man standing next to her and she decided maybe it wasn't a miracle after all. He appeared capable of most any feat. He'd heard the approach of danger before the men had even entered her house. He'd led her through those woods last night at breakneck speed without hitting the first obstacle. The light from the moon and scarce stars had been meager at best.

His auditory and visual senses were clearly far above normal. His ability to heal…

Just then, her gaze settled on his mouth. The lip that had been split last evening in his fight with Nichols had mended to the point of hardly being visible at all. The jaw that should have been bruised and swollen showed no hint of having been damaged in a fistfight. She'd seen the sheriff's right hook connect with John's jaw.

Incredible was the first word to come to mind.

She wished her father were here. He would be amazed. As a geneticist, he could fully appreciate the phenomenon. Her heart ached painfully at the thought of her father.

He'd been murdered.

She had to tell Doc, had to show him the letter. She should have told him about the taped call and the file she'd found. But her father's cautions about the security of his work had kept her silent. Clearly, she hadn't been thinking straight.

Her gaze drifted down to the rushing water below. Assuming she survived this adventure, she would tell him everything.

John led the way, carefully placing his foot on any vacant shelf created by rock or root or a combination thereof. He ensured that the chosen surface would hold his weight before proceeding. With his hands, he grasped any available protrusion with white-knuckled force.

Dani observed closely, taking his exact route, using each foothold and hand brace that he had used. She didn't think about the dank smell of the cave that lingered on her clothes or the bat droppings that were likely in her hair. Her concentration stayed fixed on the next move since her life most likely depended upon it.

The rock bit into her fingers, but she held on tightly just the same. Her legs shook with the effort of supporting her weight in such awkward positions. At times, the only available surfaces were either several feet apart or offered only inches between them. It was like a kind of vertical Twister, the game she'd loved to play back in junior high school. She almost laughed out loud when she imagined John calling out, "Right foot blue...left hand yellow."

Of course, the stakes were much higher in this game. Instead of getting all tangled up with your boyfriend as a prize, you got to live. Oh, boy, was she getting cynical or what?

The good thing about all this, she decided, was that no one could ever again accuse her of not having enough excitement in her life. She'd had sex with a complete stranger, been chased by men dressed in black combat gear, been shot at, thrown over a cliff and now she was rock climbing. Her life was a regular Club Med for the *Survivor* fanatic.

Too bad no one was paying her a million dollars for all her trouble.

Her right foot slipped.

She clutched at the rock wall.

Her breath rushed out of her lungs.

She felt her body dangling in the air a split second before her brain registered what the sensation meant. She struggled to reach her foothold once more. Couldn't. She was going to fall.

Scream, she ordered.

Nothing happened.

She felt paralyzed.

Didn't dare move…or breathe…

The rock tore into the flesh of her fingers as her weight pulled against her handholds.

She watched, helpless, as her fingers slipped, seemingly in slow motion, despite her frantic clenching.

The seconds felt like hours.

She was going to fall.

John!

He looked up just in time to see her lose her handholds.

He pushed away from the rock wall, opened his arms as he fell backward.

She slammed into him, increasing the draw of gravity, sending them both plummeting downward.

He curled around her, forming a ball a fraction of a second before they hit the water.

Cold.

They plunged deeper and deeper.

John straightened, curved his body and kicked outward, slowing their downward plunge.

He kept his left arm clutched around Dani's waist, kicking harder and harder, pushing toward the surface.

He could see the light cutting through the dark water. Could feel the temperature warming as they moved upward. The current grew stronger as they neared the surface.

Breaking into open air, he dragged Dani up next to him.

She gasped, echoing his own efforts to draw much-needed oxygen into his lungs. It took a minute for him to catch his breath. Dani required more time. She shivered uncontrollably. The water was cold. He needed to get her to the jagged shoreline on the other side. The embankment wasn't so steep on that side. They could climb it easily. Disappear into the woods. But they had to hurry. Helicopters would be out soon. John was surprised they hadn't sent out a full-scale search party already. Instinct told him that would be the next logical move. He wasn't sure how he knew this, but somehow he did. Just as he had last night…he had sensed the danger.

He frowned as he started to stroke through the water with one arm, keeping the other wrapped tightly around Dani. He didn't understand how he knew these things. He simply did. Their pursuers would be back. Soon.

Whatever this was, it was far from over.

THEY TRUDGED THROUGH the woods until dusk had settled once more. Dani couldn't remember ever feeling this exhausted. She was hungry. But at least she was dry now. Well, except for her shoes, which were still squishy. It had taken the better part of the day for her clothes to dry fully. It hadn't been that cold and the sun had been shining, but they were deep in the woods. The thick canopy of trees had blocked most of its warming rays.

She had decided hours ago that mountain climbing was vastly overrated. She now knew why she had no outdoorsy hobbies. As much as she had always loved horses, a hard-core country girl she would never make.

The smell of hay and horses was by far more pleasant than that of bat caves and murky river water. She sniffed. Though dry, she still smelled like the river.

But she was alive.

She shuddered each time she thought of falling away from that rock wall. However, John had managed to grab her and go down with her, ultimately protecting her against the impact of the water; she owed him her life.

Three times already he had rescued her.

How would she ever repay him? She'd definitely have to apologize for dragging him into this mess. He no doubt wished he'd stumbled into someone else's house. Reflecting on that idea for a bit, she decided that she'd sort of rescued him that once. But that didn't put them anywhere near even.

She stilled. Was that traffic she heard in the distance?

John stopped and looked back at her. "The highway is just over that ridge." He pointed to what she deemed east since the sun was setting in the opposite direction. "We've been moving parallel to it for a while now. Whitewater will be right over there." This time he pointed northeasterly. "About five more miles."

Whitewater. She knew Whitewater. Not a large city but big enough to have a hotel. Dammit. She didn't have any cash or a credit card. There would be restaurants and she was broke. Her stomach growled.

"Are we going to call for help there?" she wondered out loud. Surely the police would help them. They'd been shot at and chased. Her father had been murdered. Hurt sliced through her at the thought. She just couldn't believe it…couldn't believe any of it.

John's gaze locked with hers. "I don't know."

Doc. She could call Doc. He would help. "I'll call Doc," she echoed her thoughts. "He'll know what to do. He can come pick us up."

"I don't know."

John started walking again without clarifying what that meant. Why would he not trust Doc? He didn't even know the man. She'd known him her entire life.

"Doc is like family to me," she said to his back since he just kept walking.

"I need to think." He said this without a backward glance, his tone edging toward frustrated.

Wow. The man could feel frustration. The range of emotions he'd developed in the last three days blew her away. Dr. Nevin would be impressed.

The whole scenario was like watching a child develop into an adult at a highly accelerated rate. Her chest tightened with the flood of memories that hit her just then. This man was anything but a child. She had to remember that. He was a skilled lover and…dangerous.

She thought about the way he'd moved when he'd fought Nichols. The feral gleam in his eyes. But that didn't come close to what she'd heard him do to those other men in her house. It had been too dark to see but she'd heard the sounds of death. She shivered. Again she wondered who this man was. Where he had come from.

He led the way to Whitewater as if he'd lived in these mountains his entire life. He'd memorized that map, she realized. How was that possible?

Something else nagged at her. The way he'd known to catch her as she fell when she hadn't even screamed. The unnerving way he answered her questions before she asked them. An unsettling scenario started to form. Just how special was her John Doe?

It was dark before they dared venture into town. Streetlights lit the busy sidewalks. Dani had to think hard to remember what day it was. Saturday. Or was it Friday? Either way, Whitewater was bustling with activity. The local supercenter parking lot was jam-packed. A bowling alley and several fast food restaurants enjoyed plenty of business. The smell of French fries and broiling burgers scented the night air. Her stomach rumbled again.

"What're we going to do?" she asked, hurrying to catch up with John's long strides. How did he keep going? She was ready to drop.

"We're going to get a room at this hotel." He said this without slowing or even glancing her way. Most likely because it was a flat-out lie. How the hell were they supposed to get a room without cash, credit or IDs?

She peered at the brightly lit hotel that lay dead ahead. Not going to happen.

Okay, so she could fantasize about it for the next six blocks.

They entered the hotel from the rear parking area. When they reached the lobby, John waited until the desk attendant was occupied on the telephone before slipping into the corridor directly behind the front office. A sign marked Employees Only warned that they were moving into unauthorized territory. That didn't appear to faze John.

He opened door after door until he found what he was looking for. After ushering her into the office, he closed the door and turned on the light. The nameplate on the desk proclaimed the space as belonging to the manager.

A scowl moved across her face as John sat down behind the computer. "What're you doing?"

"I'm getting us a room," he informed her without taking his eyes off the computer screen. His fingers flew across the keys as if he'd been doing this for years.

Okay, so maybe her John Doe was a hotel manager.

A few more clicks and he stood. "That's it. Let's go."

Dazed and confused, Dani followed him back into the lobby. He paused to ensure that the attendant was occupied once more so that he wouldn't notice the direction from which they'd come.

"Excuse me," John said as he approached the desk.

The attendant looked up and plastered on a smile. "Yes, sir. How can I help you?" he offered in a practiced tone.

"I can't find my key."

"What name, sir?" he asked, his fingers poised on the keys of his computer.

"Daniels. Two-fifteen."

A few clicks and the attendant smiled. "It'll only take a moment, Mr. Daniels."

Daniels? From her name, she supposed. Dani. Daniels.

Less than a minute later, they had a key and were on their way to room two-fifteen. He had entered them into the system, taking up one of the unoccupied rooms, ensuring they wouldn't be disturbed.

"Where did you learn to do that?" she demanded, stunned. Relieved, but stunned.

John paused at the door numbered two-fifteen to slide the key card. He shrugged. "I wish I knew."

The statement got to Dani. It wasn't so much the way he said the words as it was the solemn expression on his face. His frustration had deepened. He wanted his memory back. He wanted his life back.

She had her own life. Why the idea of his life, one that didn't include her, made her so sad was beyond her. She had to get past this. Eventually this would be over. He would go back to wherever he'd come from and she would…go back to California and learn to get on with her life without her father.

Without John Doe.

Inside the room, Dani kicked off her shoes and rolled off her damp socks. Then she went to the bathroom and relieved herself. She'd had to once in the woods today.

Boy, had that been an experience. After she'd washed her hands she ducked her head under the faucet and had a long drink. The cool water felt good to her dry throat. Maybe it would help with her hunger as well.

She was starved.

When she exited the bathroom John was on the phone.

"Yes, this is Mr. Daniels in two-fifteen." Pause. "Yes, the key worked fine. Thank you. Listen, my wife isn't feeling well and I was wondering if the hotel restaurant would mind sending something up to the room." Another long pause. "That would be great. I'd really appreciate it. I'll check the menu and call you right back. Thanks."

Dani climbed onto the bed, watching him in morbid fascination. He was incredible and a consummate liar. "Are they really going to do that? I mean, I didn't know this chain of hotels had room service."

He smiled. The expression sent a shock quaking through her. "They don't, but I asked so nicely," he teased.

That he was kidding around with her only startled her all the more. Simply astonishing.

After they'd checked the menu and made selections, John called the desk attendant with the order. He assured John that he would personally see that the order was sent to their room as soon as possible and the charge would be assessed to their room as well.

"So, did you make up a credit card number?" she asked, curious. He had settled into one of the chairs and was surfing the television channels.

"I scanned their list of recent guests and selected one. Daniels." He glanced at her and smiled. "The name drew my attention."

She flushed, then blinked away the emotion that abruptly rose. Would her name still draw his attention when he had his real life back?

Long minutes of silence elapsed. She couldn't help wondering if he was thinking of her and…last night.

"I should call Doc," she said, pushing the thought away. She didn't want to think about life without John. It was hard to believe that she'd gotten so attached to him so quickly. She sighed. But she knew the explanation, had warned herself repeatedly. It was because of losing her father. Kind of like a rebound romance. She needed something in her life and along came John. He'd needed her. Voilà. A match made in heaven.

A knock at the door jerked both their gazes there before John could respond to her comment. He stood, crossed to answer it and she was captivated all over again by the way he moved. So sleek and fluid. As graceful as a dancer, but far more intimidating.

He checked the peephole and then opened the door to allow the waitress in with their food. He signed the bill and closed and locked the door behind the woman. The food smelled wonderful. She'd selected roast beef with potatoes. He had opted for the chicken. More of his personality coming out. For the past few days, he'd followed her lead on decisions about most everything. But tonight he'd made his own choice. She refused to consider that a bad thing.

They ate in relieved silence, a welcome atmosphere after the day's events.

When she'd cleaned her plate she set it aside and announced. "I have to call Doc. He'll be worried sick if he's gotten wind of what happened."

John remained silent for what felt like an eternity. "All right." He leaned forward, bracing his arms on his widespread knees. He looked so damned good. His hair was tousled and his clothes were wrinkled, but he looked amazing. She wanted to touch him. To feel the strength of his powerful arms around her once more. She remembered the feel of his skin, the heat of his body. The flex of every muscle as he'd made love to her. Would he make love to her again tonight?

"Dani," he began, the sound of her name on his lips making her shiver. "I don't know what any of this is about. I don't understand why this happened."

She held up a hand to stay his words. "I think it has something to do with my father. He was a scientist for the government. I—I found some…things in the past few days that made me believe that he knew something that might have cost him his life."

His gaze zeroed in on hers. "You believe your father was murdered?"

She nodded, blinking rapidly to stem the flow of tears. "He received a call shortly before his death from a former colleague. The message warned that he thought they were in trouble. Then, when I checked his mail the other day, I found a note from the same man saying that his execution had been ordered."

"Execution?" John shifted uncomfortably in his chair.

She nodded again. "This Joseph Marsh warned my father twice, but somehow he didn't get the messages or didn't heed them."

"Marsh?"

There was a tension in his voice now…a subtle shift in his posture.

"Yes." He couldn't possibly know Joseph Marsh. Perhaps the whole idea of murder and conspiracy unsettled him somehow. Certainly there would be parts of his psyche that were still unstable, vulnerable. "We don't have to talk about this, John. If it upsets you—"

"No," he said, almost sharply. "I want to hear it."

She exhaled a mighty breath and started from the beginning. She told him about the file she'd found and the phone message on the hidden tape. She'd been careful not to discuss it with anyone since her father's work was so highly classified. Then she described the letter she'd opened in her father's mail. That had changed everything.

"What exactly did your father do for the government?" he asked when she'd completed her story.

She shrugged. "I'm not really certain. It was all very secretive. He was in genetics, that I know for sure. He worked on advanced projects. I can only guess what might have been involved."

John scrubbed a hand over his face. It was the only time he'd moved since she started talking. He'd sat so very still. Like a mannequin. She didn't understand his reaction.

"And this Joseph Marsh worked with him."

"Yes. I only knew a handful of his colleagues. But I remember the name." She wished she could remember what the man looked like as well. She also wished she'd gotten to call Doc after she got the letter…but too much had happened.

John stood abruptly. Her breath caught at the sudden move. "I need a shower," he said. "Call your friend if you like." His gaze collided with hers. "If you're sure you can trust him."

"Of course I'm sure," she insisted.

He went into the bathroom and closed the door. She stared after him, feeling as if the man she had come to know and care about was gone. She didn't know this John Doe. She wasn't even sure she liked him.

She hugged her knees to her chest and fought the urge to cry. How could she have allowed herself to get this deeply involved with him? He was a stranger. That became clearer with each passing moment. She'd made a tremendous error in judgment.

But, mistake or not, she cared for him deeply.

She doubted anything could change that. He owned her heart.

Sucking in a weary breath, she dragged the phone onto the bed with her and punched in Doc's home number. She prayed he would be there. This whole situation was out of control. Way out of control. She needed Doc's help. She could no longer trust her own judgment.

Considering her past with Lane Nichols, maybe she never could.

Doc answered on the second ring.

"It's Dani," she said wistfully. "I need your help."

"Oh, sweet Jesus! You're all right! I was so afraid." He made a sound, almost a sob. "Where are you? Let me come and get you. I'll keep you safe."

He'd already heard. She clutched the phone, gathering her courage. But he couldn't know everything. "Doc, someone is trying to kill me. They came into my house—"

"I know," he cut in. "Davidson called me. Men from the government came to him in the middle of the night last night. They're looking for you, Dani. They said—"

"Men from the government are looking for me?" Why? That didn't make any sense. But then, none of this did. "I don't understand."

"Dear God, child, listen to me," Doc urged desperately. "They're not after you. They're after him. The men who broke into your house are trying to rescue you."

Dani's heart started to pound. What did he mean? No one had tried to harm her until those men came into her home. Except the friendly sheriff. "Rescue me from who? Nichols came—"

"This has nothing to do with Nichols," he interrupted, his tone practically scolding. "It's John Doe, Dani. It's him you should be running from."

"What?" That was impossible. John had saved her life twice already. Not to mention the fact that he'd rescued her from Nichols. "That's crazy."

"John Doe's real name is Adam something or other. He's an assassin for some subversive group who is trying to get at your father's files. He was sent here to kill you, Dani. Your life is in mortal danger."

Sheer terror slid through her veins like ice. "Doc, that can't be. It just…can't."

"Listen to me, child, the man was injured en route. He lost his memory. That's the only reason he hasn't completed his mission. But if he regains his full memory or even the part about his mission, he will complete it. He's a trained killer. His mission is to kill *you.*"

A kind of numbness took over, paralyzing her ability to feel anything at all. "How can you be sure…he…" She moistened her lips. "Doc, this can't be right. I can't believe he would…would even contemplate…" She couldn't say the rest. It was too crazy. Impossible. Tears slid down her cheeks. The salty droplets felt hot against her cold cheeks.

"He killed your father, Dani," Doc told her, his words shattering the last remaining vestiges of her hold on composure. "That's what Davidson told me. Those men from the government warned him that your life is in grave danger. Your father wouldn't give this Adam what he wanted, so he killed him. But his mission won't be complete until he kills you, too."

Chapter Eleven

Dani lay on her side of the bed feigning sleep for two solid hours. Beside her John or Adam—whatever his name was—finally appeared to drift off to sleep. His respiration had deepened, grown slow and steady. The tension she'd sensed in him since her call to Doc had at last relaxed.

She prayed he hadn't overheard the conversation. She distinctly remembered the shower had been running during the entire course of the call. At least, she thought it had. Doc's revelation had shocked her so that she wasn't really sure of anything anymore.

How could any of this be real?

How could her father have been murdered?

She carefully turned to stare at the man lying next to her. She shuddered with the conflicting emotions twisting inside her. How could he have done such a thing? Why would he have killed her father? Who would have ordered him to kill her? He'd…he'd made love to her. Why would he or anyone else want to hurt her and her father?

Your execution has been ordered.

The whole idea was insane…ludicrous.

Doc had to be mistaken. Those men…they must have lied.

The momentary relief she felt at reaching that conclusion died an instant death as she considered the rest of his words. Those men were from the government. Why would they lie? What purpose would it serve? Her father had been a loyal civil servant for most of his life. There was absolutely no reason for the government to turn on him.

Her gaze roamed over John's profile in the dim light cast from the bathroom. He'd left the light on and the door slightly ajar, whether from preoccupation or by design she couldn't say. Her heart contracted painfully when she even toyed with the idea that he could be a murderer.

But there were things—facts—that she'd witnessed with her own eyes that lent credibility to the concept. The transformation when he'd fought with Nichols. He'd morphed into some sort of fighting machine. His eyes had reflected a savagery unlike any she'd ever seen. As a physician in a large metropolitan hospital, she'd seen her share of psychotic behavior, but this was far more brutal, more threatening than any she'd experienced. The way he moved, with extreme fluidity and immense strength.

He'd raced through the woods in utter darkness and taken risks only a highly trained expert would. Jumping over that cliff, falling back into that river. It wasn't that she didn't believe that most caring humans wouldn't have attempted such feats to save another's life as well as their own; it was the way he executed the moves...with precision and confidence. He had known what he was doing. Then she thought of the way he'd hacked into the hotel's computer system. He was expertly trained on more than one level.

A new stab of fear pierced her. None of those things explained his heightened senses, his incredible ability to heal injuries in a matter of mere hours.

She'd been so overwhelmed with the loss of her father...so intensely alone, she'd overlooked a great deal of glaring and bizarre facts related to her John Doe.

He was no normal man.

She blinked and drew in a heavy breath. It went against the grain for her to even acknowledge the concept. As a trained physician, she based her conclusions on scientific fact, on tangible evidence. She simply did not believe in unearthly miracles or any other hypothesis that would be even loosely called science fiction.

However, she had seen the tangible evidence... touched it. This was real. *He* was real. And so were his phenomenal physical abilities.

The question was, had he come to her home to kill her? Had he killed her father? Another memory pinged her already emotionally raw senses. He'd stared at pictures of her father for hours on end and questioned her about him. She'd seen the recognition flare briefly in his eyes as he did so. Every instinct insisted that he had known her father on some level. But did that make him a cold-blooded killer? Had his loss of memory been the only thing standing between him killing her and him saving her?

Lastly, Dani considered the way he'd made love to her. She'd led him the first time, drawn him into the bone-melting heat at his insistence to understand. But he had taken the lead after that. He had tortured her to the point of insanity. Had made her beg for him to finish it. Would none of that matter when he remembered his real mission?

Would the realization that she'd given herself completely, heart and soul, to him make no difference? Was he that kind of ruthless assassin?

She closed her eyes and pushed the thoughts and images away. She refused to believe that he had killed her father. She simply could not make her brain grasp the idea. There had to be a mistake.

Still, could she take the chance? Could she carry on as if Doc had not said those things to her and hope for the best? No. She couldn't. If this man—her chest constricted—had killed her father, she wanted him to pay for that senseless crime.

She cursed herself for being a fool. How could she harbor any feelings for the man who may have murdered her father? Then again, how could she have given herself so completely to someone without those very feelings?

Firming her resolve, Dani scooted carefully from the bed, praying she would not wake him. Doc had told her to wait until she felt she could escape and then to run like hell. He promised that two of the men from the government would be waiting for her only two blocks away in the rear parking area of an all-night pancake house. She was to look for a gray sedan with the sun visors turned down.

The men would take her to safety. Another team would enter the hotel room and take John into custody.

At the door of their hotel room, she hesitated. She told her traitorous heart not to look back, but she just couldn't help herself. She had to look at him one last time. Her entire body stupidly cried out for his touch. She should have better control than this, especially with what she knew.

Furious with herself, she eased the door open and slipped from the room. In a few more minutes, it would all be over and she would finally learn the truth.

Maybe then she could get on with her life.

John lay still until she'd exited the room, then he jumped from the bed. Moving swiftly, he pulled on his jeans and shoes, then his shirt. He couldn't let her get too far ahead of him.

Fully dressed, he quietly left the room and visually searched the exterior balcony that ran the length of the building with exit stairs at each end and the parking area beyond. She was halfway to the street, moving quickly. He took the stairs at the west end and went after her, taking care not to get too close.

He had overheard the final part of her conversation with her friend. He'd stepped out of the shower and cracked open the door only narrowly but he could hear just fine. The man had warned her to run, had told her that he had been ordered to kill her.

John scowled at the idea. A part of him denied the accusation, but another part, something deep inside him that he couldn't pull to the surface just yet, warned that the accusation held some merit.

The idea of hurting her slashed through him like a hot blade. No way. He would never hurt Dani. He... cared for her very much. Needed her. Wanted her.

Her friend, Doc, she called him, had told her to meet two of the men who'd come to him with this news in a parking lot not far away. He remembered seeing the pancake house.

John didn't need a flashing neon light to know a setup when he heard one. Dani was too trusting. Maybe her friend really believed he was helping her, maybe not. Whatever the case, she would be walking into a trap. John sensed it on every level. He had learned to trust his instincts in the past twenty-four hours. Whatever he had done before losing his memory, whoever he was, he knew this sort of business all too well.

Though he had no weapon, he would do whatever it took to protect Dani from the men her friend had sent. If, as he suggested, another team planned to descend upon the hotel room, they would find it empty.

Dani's progress didn't slow, though her movements grew more cautious as she reached the rear of the building her friend had cited as the rendezvous. John remained in the shadows, using whatever cover he could to stay as close to her as possible. When she spotted the gray sedan, his only option was a nearby refuse bin. He slipped to the end of the huge metal box, flattening against the dark green surface and listening intently.

"Miss Archer?"

The two men had exited the car. They wore suits and looked every bit the part of government agents. But an alarm had gone off in John's head the instant he got a visual on the two. He couldn't say he recognized them, but his gut told him they were bad guys. Really bad guys.

"Yes." Dani's voice quaked with fear. "Are the others at the hotel room already?" she asked, dredging up a little bravado. "Doc assured me they wouldn't harm John until—"

"His name is Adam, Miss Archer, and he's a killer," one of the men interrupted. "I wouldn't worry about him if I were you."

"I just don't know," she said brokenly.

John had to restrain the urge to go to her. Then he frowned. He hadn't heard the part where she'd insisted that he not be harmed. Hearing the words now gave him hope that she didn't completely believe the accusation.

Adam.

He rolled the name over in his head and something clicked. It felt right. Adam. He could be this Adam they spoke of. But that didn't make him a killer. He thought of how badly he'd wanted to kill that sheriff who'd manhandled Dani...but that was because he'd threatened Dani. That didn't make him a murderer.

"We'll need you to come with us, Miss Archer," the second man said.

She fell back a step as if uncertain. "I…I don't know if this is such a good idea. Maybe I should go back to the hotel."

Tell them to forget it, John urged silently. *Tell them to get lost.*

The gun was in the man's hand in a heartbeat. The taller of the two. The one who looked to be in charge. John barely resisted the urge to throw himself between Dani and the armed man. No sudden moves, he warned the part of him that had gone stupid with fear and fury.

"Get in the car, Miss Archer," the man ordered. He had the vaguest accent. South American maybe. John couldn't be sure. He looked remotely Latin. But the lighting was too poor to be certain. A couple of nearby streetlights provided the only illumination.

As Dani stumbled away another step in terror, John's own terror ratcheted up a notch. *Don't move, baby,* he urged with all his mental powers. *Don't move. Be very, very still.*

She tensed…almost as if she'd heard him.

He silently repeated the mantra just in case.

"Don't make us do this here," the other man said. He'd drawn his weapon as well now. "We don't want to hurt you. All we want is the file."

File?

Dani looked stunned.

"What file?" she demanded with renewed strength. John smiled. Maybe she had sensed his presence. Good. Because he wasn't going to let anything happen to her.

"Don't give me that phony innocent stuff," the tall

one said. "You made the call. We know you have the file. Now where is it?"

"Give us the location now and you won't end up dead like your old man," the shorter of the two suggested cruelly.

Dani sucked in a sharp breath. "You…you killed my father?"

Tall man shook his head. "We didn't have to, his colleague did. A man he trusted."

Dani wagged her head side to side in denial, her body trembled with the impact of the man's words. He had to be talking about Joseph Marsh…but she couldn't believe John could have been associated with her father. She just didn't know. "I don't understand any of this. What kind of file could my father have that would cost him his life?"

The short one laughed, the sound echoing haughtily. "You don't know, do you?" He looked at his friend. "They think she's some kind of Judas and she doesn't even know what the hell this is about." He laughed again. "How freaking ironic. That's just like Center to screw up something so simple."

Center. John tensed. The word went through him like a bullet tearing through his skull and lodging in his brain. He understood Center. Knew Center. His gut cramped and his head swam slightly before he grabbed back control. Focus, he ordered. Dani needed him.

"What's Center?" she asked, her confusion visible along with the fear running rampant inside her.

"It's the place where your friend Adam came from.

He was created there by scientists like your father," the tall man said. "Now get in the car." The last was a savage growl.

Dani felt the shock like a ten on the Richter scale. John—Adam—had been created by her father? That was completely nuts. Impossible. Her conviction left her in a furious rush. Genetics. Her father specialized in genetics. His projects were so secret hardly anyone knew about his work. He spent most of his time in some secret place out west. Colorado, she thought.

The readying click of a weapon shattered the silence, jerking her attention back to the two men holding guns aimed directly at her.

They were going to kill her. She summoned her scattered courage. "I'm sorry to disappoint you, gentlemen, but I don't know anything about my father's work." She shook her head, hysteria bubbling up in her throat as she considered her plight. "I mean, really, I know absolutely nothing about it. I don't even know what he worked on all those years."

The two men exchanged wary glances. "All we want is the file," the taller one said. He looked Latin, she decided. Latin and lethal, now that he had a gun in his hand.

"Just tell us where it is and we'll let you live," the shorter, heavier one reiterated.

Likely story, she concluded. Her father was dead. Someone had murdered him for his work. Certainly these men would never allow her to live. Her first assessment had been right. She'd seen their faces. Letting her walk away wasn't an option. Even she knew better than that. It happened all the time on television crime dramas and in the movies.

"I guess you'll just have to kill me," she said, surrendering to the inevitable. "I don't know anything about any…file." The image of her father's upright Hoover vacuum cleaner suddenly zoomed into vivid 3-D focus. The file. The digital storage stick. Joseph Marsh. *I think we're in trouble. Your execution has been ordered.* "Oh, God," she murmured.

The two men swapped uncertain looks once more.

"I guess this means you've remembered something significant," the Latin guy suggested smugly. "How convenient for you." He gestured to the car with his gun. "Now get in the damned car. You can regale us with your revelations en route."

She shook her head. "It's not what you think. It's…it's nothing." Even she didn't believe that feeble rebuttal. The file had to be something or it wouldn't have been hidden. She simply didn't understand it. Surely that tiny stick with its meager contents hadn't cost her father his life!

"All right, lady, enough stalling. Let's go," the short guy ordered.

Lie down on the ground.

Dani jumped, startled.

The order hadn't come from either of the men. It came from inside her head. *Lie down on the ground. Now!* She'd heard it before… *Don't move… Be very still. On the ground!* the voice ordered.

She dropped like a rock, sprawling onto the asphalt then curling into a ball. "Help!" she screamed. Screaming hadn't been part of the order, but what the hell? It felt right.

"Shut up, you stupid bitch!" The tall guy swore repeatedly as he tried to drag her to her feet.

Dani screamed again. A swift slap shut her up. The other guy grabbed her by the hair. "Get up!" he growled from between clenched teeth.

The two men's heads suddenly slammed together. Skulls cracked. She blinked as they silently crumpled around her. She scrambled away. What the…?

John reached for her. "Are you all right?"

She gasped. The realization that he was actually there…that it had been his voice screaming orders inside her head suddenly kicked her in the gut like an ornery mule.

She blinked, her eyes burning, her jaw stinging. *Adam. Center. He killed your father.*

"Stay away from me," she warned, fury whipping through her like a hurricane.

"Dani, please, we have to hurry," he urged, easing closer. "Others may be coming."

Her head shook from side to side. Her entire body started to tremble once more. "No. You're…you're… I don't know who you are."

He sighed, those relentless blue eyes compelling her to trust him. He manacled her arm with one powerful hand. "We don't have time for this."

She dug in her heels and pounded him with her free hand. "Let me go!" Her efforts were useless against him.

He opened the driver's side door of a gray sedan and shoved her inside. Quickly hitting the lock button, he scooted in behind the wheel and slammed the door shut before she could scramble to the other side. The engine started and he barreled backward, propelling her against the dash.

"Buckle up," he ordered.

Dani stared at the determined expression on his face. She swallowed back the panic climbing yet again into her throat. Her fingers fumbled for the seat belt. She had no choice…she was a prisoner.

She flicked one last glance at the two men lying motionless on the asphalt before her captor rocketed onto the street. They would have killed her, she had no doubt. Her gaze shifted to the man behind the wheel. If there were any truth to their story, he would as well.

She snapped the buckle into place. Well, she thought numbly, better the devil she knew…

But, then again, she didn't really know him at all.

"YOU FAILED."

O'Riley stared at the man across the conference table who had come all the way from Washington, D.C., to state the obvious. "I'm not finished yet," he said calmly, determined not to make this any worse than it already was.

All but two members of the team he'd sent to the Archer ranch were dead. And if their latest intel was correct, a move had been made by the other side to intercept Adam and his companion.

Damn Marsh and Thurlo. They had joined forces with the other side. That was clear now. The only question was, how much did the others know?

"I want a detailed strategy, not idle promises," U.S. Congressman Terrence Winslow, head of the Collective, a watchdog group the president himself had commissioned to oversee Center activities. Thurlo had been a part of that group as well. Unlike Donald Thurlo, Joseph Marsh had served as project manager at Center, putting him in a hands-on position. He was the real threat, knew far too much.

O'Riley exhaled a heavy breath. Hell, he might as well tell the man. He would know soon enough anyway. "Adam has been compromised," he confessed. "We don't know the extent of the damage. We had hoped to bring him in alive, but that may not be possible."

Winslow's eyes bulged. He, of all people, knew the ramifications of any sort of security infraction. That an Enforcer had been compromised was the worst-case scenario. "What the hell are you doing about it?"

He'd only just made the decision. He had little choice. Dupree had learned that another group had approached the Virginia State Police investigator named Davidson. They'd left him for dead, but he'd survived. Only two hours ago, he had regained consciousness in a Richmond hospital and told the story. O'Riley had suspected the involvement of one particularly sadistic group, but confirmation was vital. This was no longer about a simple internal violation of security protocol. This had gone way beyond that now. This was a Level IV national security breach.

"I'm sending in Cain," O'Riley said, bracing himself for the repercussions. "It will take an Enforcer to stop one."

"Are you mad?" Winslow roared. "Cain is not on operational status. You know that!"

O'Riley forced a calm he didn't feel. "Cain is the only Enforcer we have capable of stopping Adam. No one else could even come close." Admittedly, Cain was only used in the most extreme situations. The situation definitely met those criteria.

Winslow struggled to regain his own composure. "Give me a current status on Cain."

"We have every reason to believe that he's reached the tolerable range," O'Riley flat-out lied. "His latest assessments are very strong."

Cain was the prototype, the original Enforcer. He had been created while the program had still been under the guidance of Dr. Waylon Galen. Galen had been the inspirational genius behind the theory that the human species could be greatly enhanced through gene manipulation. His work had resulted in a number of unparalleled enhancements to the first human experiment—Cain. There had been only one drawback to Galen's achievements; he had left out one critical element—emotion. His creation was, for all intents, devoid of all basic human emotions such as compassion. Cain felt only a single-minded determination to accomplish his goal.

Daniel Archer had spotted that defect early in the process. An upwardly mobile scientific genius then, he had insisted that changes needed to be made. Galen had gone ballistic and argued that he was in charge. The Collective had deemed him wrong and Archer right. Galen had exited the program in a snit, only to die one year later, a recluse from society.

Overcoming the resulting five-year setback, Archer had salvaged the program. He was the one who had taken Project Eugenics from a diamond in the rough to a shining star. Where Galen had been a genius, Archer had been something well beyond that mere label. His work defied accurate description. As wondrous as his work was, if his findings were ever to fall into the wrong hands, the entire world would be at great risk. The Collective, as the controlling entity of Center, had deemed itself sole watchdog over the project.

Now, everything was at risk.

They had to find that encrypted key code file before the others, the Concern. Only the Concern knew the project existed. No one else would have the courage to attempt going up against the Collective. The code contained in the missing file would unlock the secrets of the project foolishly stored in Archer's personal files. It had to be found and destroyed or locked away at Center. Any risk was acceptable. The game had moved to a whole new level with Archer's phenomenal success.

Only one Enforcer's skills rivaled Adam's. Only one possessed the single-minded determination to defy failure.

Cain.

Chapter Twelve

Dani awoke with a start.

She looked around, confused.

It was dark. The wipers slashed back and forth across the windshield, slinging the falling rain away from the glass.

Her gaze landed on the driver.

John…Adam.

She blinked.

How could she have fallen asleep? She shook off the lingering drowsiness and stared out at the dark landscape to get her bearings.

She wouldn't ask where they were or what his destination was because she didn't want to hear his voice. Didn't want to talk to him. She drew in a breath, her chest tight.

If it were true—if he'd killed her father—he had to pay for that. No matter that he had saved her life over and over again, she couldn't forgive him. Her father hadn't deserved to die. He had been a good man. She squeezed her eyes shut to block the gruesome images that accompanied the thought. The idea that someone had pushed him off that roof or committed a violent act against him that resulted in similar injuries was more than she could bear to consider.

Had he recognized his killer? Had he known death was coming? Is that why this man had been fascinated with pictures of her father? Had he known somehow that there was a connection? That he had wielded the ultimate power over a man twice his age and far less physically able to protect himself?

"Stop the car!" She had to get out. Walk. Scream. Something.

He didn't hesitate. He braked to a stop, easing onto the side of the road.

Dani shoved the door open and scrambled out into the damp night. She tore out across an open field. She didn't care. She just had to move…had to run. The rain pelted her skin, blurred her vision but she kept going. She didn't look back but she didn't have to. He was right behind her. She felt his presence as surely as her own heartbeat. How had she allowed such a bond to form? Where was her common sense…her good judgment?

Her father was dead and she'd fallen for the man who might be his killer. How sick was that? She'd had sex with a man she didn't even know. Had allowed him to drag her into this insanity. Or maybe she'd already been there and simply hadn't realized it yet. After all, this was about her father and his work.

Part of her resisted…wanted to believe Adam innocent.

The man's words about Adam echoed inside her head...*he was created there by men like your father.*

She stumbled, her feet tangling in the ankle-deep wet grass, then stalled. As a physician she was well aware of the advancements in genetic engineering...the hope of how designer genetics could improve the quality of life. She knew all the good that could come of that kind of research on a global scale. But as a woman, she simply could not come to terms with the idea of creating superhumans for use as security or military personnel. For the love of God, how else would they use genetically enhanced men like Adam? She'd witnessed his skill at taking down the enemy. She didn't even want to imagine his performance level under normal circumstances.

Her breath gushed in and out of her lungs. She wanted to cry...to curse men who would allow research to go that far...to play God.

Men like her father.

Dani dropped to her knees and doubled over, unable to hold back the sobs churning inside her.

How could her father do that? What had he been thinking? Genetic enhancements should only serve to improve quality of life, not to create designer humans. When had he become one of them? One of those scientists who had no scruples when it came to tampering with creation?

If she believed any of this, she had to admit that he'd played God and it had gotten him killed. Now those same people were after her.

The tears burned her eyes…the sobs tore at her chest, ripped from her throat. She hadn't known her father any more than she knew the man hovering over her.

She turned her face up to the sky, allowed the rain to pour over her like angels' tears. This was wrong…so wrong. She didn't want to know it…didn't want to believe it.

Adam…John…*he* dropped down beside her and reached for her, but she avoided his touch. "Leave me alone!" She scrubbed at her face, then hugged her arms around her middle. Her clothes had plastered to her skin, but she didn't care. Her head moved side to side in perpetual denial. "Just go away," she muttered.

"I can't leave you here," he said softly, as if he gave a damn.

She glared at him. Despite the drizzling rain, the partially hidden moon provided enough light for her to see the intensity of those vivid blue eyes. He wanted her to believe his words…wanted her to trust him. No way. He'd come here to kill her. The realization knifed through her all over again.

"Why don't you just do it now and get it over with?" she demanded, hurling the words at him like spears.

He searched her face, fat drops of rain slipping down his face, but he didn't seem to notice. "Do what?"

The sincerity…the utter innocence of the question was like salt in her wounds. She'd watched him kill those men with his bare hands. He was certainly capable of doing the job armed or not—whether he remembered or not. "They sent you to kill me. Just do it! Get it over with!" Her voice sounded too high-pitched. She didn't care. "Killing me should be even easier than killing my father." She flung out her arms, offering her chest and throat to him. A single well-placed blow to either vulnerable area could kill a person. No weapon required. A killer—assassin—would know that better than she would.

The steady drizzle had glued his shirt to his chest, displaying those powerful muscles and yet he looked completely harmless. Even vulnerable.

That's what he wanted her to see. She couldn't trust herself…couldn't believe her own eyes anymore.

"I didn't kill your father." The words whispered through the thick tension between them. "He was my friend. I'm not sure how I know that, but I do."

She blocked the emotion welling inside her at his seemingly genuine tone. "In any event," she insisted, "you did come here to kill me. That part's true, isn't it?"

He looked away for a moment and the bottom dropped out of her stomach. It was true. She'd thought it couldn't hurt any worse, but it did.

"I can't be sure," he offered hesitantly, "but I think it's possible. I recognized the Center those men spoke of. I know the term has something to do with where I work or live or both." He shrugged. "That's all I remember."

Dani scrubbed the commingled tears and rain from her face and leveled her gaze on his. "What's to keep you from completing your mission if your memory comes back?"

He swallowed hard. She watched with desperate longing as the muscles of his throat worked. She'd reveled in how wonderfully made he was and now she knew why…he *was* the perfect man. Science had ensured that he had no flaws.

"I can't explain." He released a heavy breath, his expression turning even more impossibly vulnerable. "But hurting you would be like hurting myself. I don't know where I end and you begin…you feel like a part of me."

His voice. She'd heard him warning her when she'd faced those two men in that parking lot. She wasn't so sure she actually believed in psychic connections but she'd definitely heard him speaking to her…telling her to get down.

"That may only be temporary," she countered, determined not to fall into what could be a trap. She shivered, the cold suddenly penetrating the despair that had cloaked her.

He reached for her again. This time, she didn't have the wherewithal to dodge his touch. Steady hands encircled her arms and he tugged her closer to him.

"I will protect you, Dani. Please believe that."

She wanted to. Oh, how she wanted to. But she'd loved and trusted her father and hadn't even really known him. How could she trust this man?

She shivered again, unable to stop the reaction that resulted as much from his touch as from the cold rain invading her bones. "I don't know if I can do that."

He moved closer. Wrapped those strong arms around her. "Let me take you home. We'll be safe there."

She drew away from that welcoming embrace and looked up at him, startled at the suggestion. "But those men—"

"Have already been there," he finished for her. "They won't expect us to go back."

Incredibly, his proposal made sense. They had to go somewhere. Neither of them had any money. Accessing accounts or credit cards would give away their location. At least at the ranch, they would have shelter and food. And dry clothes. She shivered again.

"Okay," she surrendered. "Take me home."

WHEN THEY REACHED the long drive that led to the Archer ranch, Adam left Dani in the car and went ahead to scout out the area. If anyone was waiting at the house, he wanted to discover that fact alone.

To his relief, the house was empty and so were the barn and garage. He made his way back to the car. Fortunately it had stopped raining. Another good thing. When he reached the car, he slid behind the wheel. "They're gone," he told her to put her mind at ease.

She nodded without looking at him. She still didn't trust him and he didn't blame her. He wasn't sure he trusted himself.

He let her out at the house and parked the car in the garage with Daniel Archer's sedan, then closed the overhead door. Dani had already gone upstairs by the time he got to the house. He moved up the stairs, considering all the men had said. Center. He knew Center. Adam. The name felt right. It was the other that didn't bode well. His gut told him that he had not killed Daniel Archer, that he was a trusted friend. Yet, Dani was another story. His instincts failed when it came to her. The attraction he felt to her—the bond—overwhelmed everything else.

The shower was running in her bathroom. He hesitated before leaving the room, his attention settling on the tousled sheets of the bed. He inhaled deeply, still able to smell the lingering scent of their lovemaking. He closed his eyes and remembered the urgency, the mind-blowing sensations. Her pull tugged at him even now. He wanted to join her in the shower, wanted to hold her and comfort her with his body. He desperately needed to hear her cry out for him as release claimed her. She was his...he would protect her. Nothing in his past would change that.

The spray of water stopped and his head came up just as she stepped out of the shower. She'd left the door open. He hadn't meant to intrude. She grabbed her towel and held it to her chest to cover her body.

Too late—the image was seared into his brain. "When you're dressed, gather whatever you need," he told her. "We'll sleep in the barn."

Confusion lined her brow. "The barn?"

He nodded. "*If* they come back for some reason, they'll look here first."

Adam went into the guest room bath and stripped off his clothes and showered quickly. He pulled on a clean pair of jeans and another of the T-shirts she'd told him had belonged to her father. He thought about the face in the photographs and tried hard to remember something about the man. That fleeting sense of trust and camaraderie was all he could grasp. There was more, but it was just out of reach.

He shook off the sensations and went in search of Dani. They needed blankets, food and water. A flashlight would be good. He also needed to know if her father had a weapon. If he'd been thinking clearly, he would have taken one or both of the guns the men in the parking lot had been carrying. But he'd been too focused on getting Dani to safety. That didn't feel right. He sensed that he generally performed better than that. The injuries the neurologist had spoken of had obviously left their undeniable mark.

Dani was no longer in her room. She wasn't anywhere upstairs. He hurried down the stairs, worry gnawing at his gut. What if she'd decided she couldn't trust him? He stilled at the final step and concentrated hard. No. She was still here. He could feel her presence. There was a connection between them that he was sure he had never before experienced. It meant something special. He couldn't label it, but he was determined not to lose it.

He found her in the den. She'd started a small fire with crumpled paper and a shoebox she had torn to pieces.

"What is that?"

She looked up at him, resignation dulling her eyes. She held out her hand. A small object, a couple inches long, black in color, lay in her palm. "This," she said with more strength than he would have guessed she possessed at that moment, "is what got my father killed." She tossed the object into the fire, then picked up a minicassette and pitched it into the flames as well. "That, too," she added, staring into the quickly dying flames. She tore off a couple more strips of cardboard and fueled the fire.

Adam considered the small black object, his mind searching for identification, and then he knew. A digital storage stick used in digital cameras and other electronic devices.

The file.

"That was the file those men were looking for?" He moved to her side and piled the rest of the cardboard and a few more wadded pages of paper to the fire. Whatever it contained, no one would be able to use it now.

She nodded, her expression grim. "Pathetic, isn't it? My father died because of what was on that tiny object." She looked at Adam then, her gaze so forlorn that it made his chest ache. "Hardly seems fair. He devoted his entire life to research, supposedly for the betterment of mankind, and in the end his life wasn't even as valuable as the file on that little plastic stick."

"We should get out to the barn," he offered, hoping to get her beyond the moment.

She nodded and allowed him to assist her to her feet. He watched a moment to ensure the fire died. Together they gathered the blankets and other supplies they would need.

In the kitchen, he hesitated before going out the back door. "Is there a weapon in the house?"

She shook her head. "My father didn't believe in guns."

Adam nodded. "All right." He led her through the night, not bothering with a flashlight until they were inside the barn. Nor did he question the realization that he now thought of himself as Adam rather than John.

The horses greeted them with snorts and shuffling of hooves. Dani pitched her load aside to go immediately to first one and then the other and smooth a hand over their gleaming forelocks.

Adam chose an unoccupied stall near the rear of the barn, heaped up some straw there and spread their blankets atop the generous pile. Once he'd deposited their supplies nearby, he located the closest egress route—a side door at the rear of the stables made for access to the attached corral. It was wide enough for one to lead a horse through, but wasn't a double door like the set at the front. He checked to ensure it opened without squeaking, then closed it once more.

"We should get some sleep now."

She looked up at him from the horse currently on the receiving end of her attention. "I think I'd like to sleep over here." She gestured to an empty stall on the opposite side of the barn's long center aisle.

"I don't think that's a good idea. We need to stay together."

Looking clearly defeated, she didn't argue further. Instead, she moved across the aisle and settled on the pallet he'd made. He sat down next to her and clicked off the flashlight. He placed it next to her. "If you need it, it's right there." His vision adjusted quickly to the darkness.

"Thank you." Her voice sounded stilted. He wished he could take the worry away from her, but he wasn't sure that was possible.

He lay back and closed his eyes. He needed rest. His body was tired and so was his mind. He'd slept very little in the past three days. He couldn't protect her if he allowed himself to continue on this course. Sleep was essential to function.

'For a long while, she didn't move. Finally, she lay down next to him, careful not to touch him.

Adam drew in her sweet scent with every breath he took. Despite his exhaustion, his body reacted. He wanted to touch her but didn't dare. She needed her distance right now. He sensed her desperation to reason all that she'd seen and heard. But he feared there would be no reason that would satisfy her. She'd lost too much…no longer trusted herself, much less anyone else.

He wished he knew how to assuage that kind of hurt. Perhaps there was no relief for such a loss. He had never lost anyone, he realized with complete certainty. He had no basis from which to form a conclusion. Yet whatever caused her pain caused him pain. Also something new.

Sleep came slowly for him, as it did for the woman next to him. Though they never touched, they shared the relentless agony of loss. He hoped she could feel how much he wanted to comfort her. With his last thought before surrendering to sleep, he wished he could hold her.

HIS FINGERS wrapped around her throat. She stared up at him, brown eyes wide in disbelief…in horror.

"No," she whimpered before he cut off her ability to speak…to breathe.

To deprive the body of oxygen was a slow, terrifying death. He would not make her wait so long. Instead, his fingers clamped more tightly around her throat, crushing the fragile bones…collapsing the delicate windpipe and larynx…damaging the vital arteries. Death came far more quickly and with little or no resistance. She had surrendered without a fight.

His mission was complete.

Adam jerked upright. His heart thundered in his chest. Sweat ran down his forehead.

Dani.

He grabbed her, pulled her to him so that he could examine her in the near darkness. The movement startled her and she shrieked and tried to tear away from his hold.

He exhaled the breath he'd been holding. She was safe. Safe. He released her and closed his eyes. Dreaming. He'd only been dreaming. He scrubbed his hands over his face and through his hair. He'd dreamed of killing her…of completing his mission.

What if she was right?

What if she couldn't trust him?

He wasn't a normal human…who knew what had been done to him? He could very well act without thought.

His fingers fisted in his hair and anguish roared through him. He was a killer. They had sent him here to execute her. If he failed, they would send others. It was not speculation, but absolute certainty radiating from some part of his memory that struggled to reach the surface.

"Are you…okay?"

Her voice sounded every bit as weary as it had last night. Weary and fragile. She needed protecting and he was no longer sure he could do the job.

He took a deep breath and pulled himself together. "Yes," he lied. "Are you okay?" He looked at her then in the dim light of dawn reaching through the skylights overhead.

"I don't know."

He understood.

"Did you have a nightmare?"

He considered lying again, but didn't see the point. "Yes."

"What was it about?"

He hadn't expected that.

"About me?" she guessed.

He nodded.

She looked away. "What do we do now?"

"I need to take you someplace safe."

"I thought we were safe here," she ventured. He could hear the rising uncertainty in her voice.

"We are. Probably. But I didn't mean safe from *them*." He closed his eyes and said the rest. "I meant some place safe from *me*."

Her silence told him she understood.

For a long while, they left it that way. What was there to say? She was right to be afraid of him. He wanted to protect her, but feared that his memory would come surging back and that he might kill her before he could stop himself. Too vivid scenes from the nightmare flashed through his mind. He shuddered.

She took his hand in hers and sighed. "I think I'll take my chances with you."

He turned to look at her and something shifted in his chest. The longing was unbearable. He had to touch her with his hands…his mouth.

Dani knew he was going to kiss her and she didn't stop him. She wanted his kiss. Needed the contact. He didn't let her down. He kissed her long and hard, until her whole body hummed with desire. Her arms went up and around his neck and, slowly, they fell back onto the blankets together.

He didn't take it beyond holding her and kissing her, not that she would have resisted. But it was enough. The feel of his powerful body next to hers and his strong arms around her was all the comfort she needed.

Then and there she admitted defeat. Whether he'd been sent to kill her or not, she wanted to be with him. He was all she had to hang on to. Her father was gone. She couldn't risk exposing Doc to any more of this. Those men could have killed him; instead, they had used her dear friend. She had to try and keep Doc out of this. Adam was all she had. And she wasn't about to let go.

CAIN SURVEYED the parking lot behind the pancake house. Blue lights throbbed insistently. Yellow crime scene tape fluttered in the breeze. A crowd of onlookers stood back the required distance, murmuring and pointing, all looking shocked and sickened by the sight of two dead men.

Adam's aftermath was very much out of character. Cain's colleague was generally much more subtle than this. The incident lent credence to reports of Adam's deteriorating condition.

Cain's cell phone vibrated, drawing his attention from the scene. He opened the phone and pressed it to his ear, didn't bother with a greeting. "They're gone," he announced. Simple, to the point. Anything else would be a waste of words.

"Find them," O'Riley ordered. He was growing desperate. The urgency in his tone gave away his proximity to the edge. "Eliminate them both…if necessary."

Cain closed his phone and put it away without responding. He would find them. That wasn't a problem. He knew exactly how Adam would react to the situation. Since he was injured on some level, he would seek safety.

Safety in this instance could mean only one place.

Cain knew precisely where.

Chapter Thirteen

Dani considered calling Doc and letting him know that she was all right. But then she decided that calling him might not be such a good idea. The less he knew, the better off he would be. She'd lost her father; she didn't want to lose the man who'd been like an uncle to her as well. He was the only family she had left. The enemy, whoever the hell they were, had already used him once to try and get to her.

Adam agreed to a venture into the house. A hot breakfast would do them both good. It was daylight now; it wasn't as if they wouldn't see the enemy coming. She stirred the scrambled eggs. Adam would hear anyone approaching the house. She wondered then if he actually heard the sound or if he sensed an intruder's presence.

There were so many things she wanted to know about him. Now that she'd gotten over the initial shock, part of her yearned to learn more about her father's work. She still felt strongly that morally and ethically the creation of humans for any sort of research was wrong. Yet, she would be lying if she didn't admit to being intrigued. The idea that her father had been able to make that happen was…startling.

She raked the eggs onto a plate and checked the toast. No sooner had the thought occurred to her than the slices popped up; the smell of hot, browned bread filled the room. Handling the slices gingerly, she stacked them onto a pile next to the eggs. Juice, coffee and they'd be set.

She closed her eyes and stood very still for a few moments. Her emotions were on a roller coaster ride, up and down. Part of her angry, another awed. Her feelings for Adam or John or whoever he was warred with her most basic beliefs in what was right and wrong…it was too much to process just now. Too many variables to come to a sensible conclusion. She needed time. She opened her eyes once more. But time was their enemy.

Right now, she needed to eat. Turning to the table, her gaze collided with a steady gray one. The plate in her hand fell to the floor and shattered in a dozen ceramic shards, its contents flying in all directions.

A scream rushed into her throat but lodged there, as every muscle in her body froze in terror.

The man was very tall. Strong-looking. Broad shoulders. Muscular arms bulged beneath the navy pullover sweater he wore. Jeans, hiking boots. The same kind of hiking boots Adam had been wearing when she found him. Her gaze jerked upward, but stalled before reaching his face. He held a black gun in his hand, the business end aimed at her.

"Don't move," he warned, his voice low and as cold as ice.

She blinked, hoping she had somehow imagined him. He wasn't like the men from last night. He was... he was like Adam. An intensity emanated from his eyes and though he stood perfectly still, there was an energy about him. It hummed around his being, vibrated the very air.

"Who are you?" The words were scarcely a whisper, more a spoken thought. She hadn't even realized she'd said them until the fragile sound echoed in the room.

Before the man could reply, Adam suddenly appeared behind him, a rifle in his hand. Where had he gotten that gun? Confusion whirled with the fear playing havoc with Dani's equilibrium. Bright pinpoints of light flashed before her eyes. She recognized the symptoms. *Not now. Don't pass out. Keep it together,* she ordered.

She braced herself against the counter. Two sets of eyes focused on the movement.

"Who are you?" Adam repeated.

"You know who I am," the other man said.

His voice made her tremble. If she had ever heard a more threatening, more emotionless sound, she couldn't recall the event. His hair was dark...almost black. He wore it longer than Adam's. He stood maybe an inch taller as well. But they had the same powerful build... the same flawless face. And those eyes. Piercing... analyzing.

He was one of them.

Dani swallowed back the emotions clogging her throat. This man had come from wherever Adam had been created. Center, the men from last night had said.

But there was something different about this man.

He was cold…not like Adam.

Why was he here?

And then she knew.

He had come to complete the mission Adam had failed to finish.

He was her executioner.

Adam propped the gun against the back of the intruder's skull. "Who…are…you?" he demanded through gritted teeth.

"Put the gun down, Adam," he ordered, dead calm.

Dani wanted to do something to stop this from escalating out of control. She could feel some twisted fate sucking them into a vortex of doom. This man would kill her and probably Adam, too. Adam was no longer perfect, no longer one of them. He would be a loose end now…nothing more.

Adam began to move. Her breath trapped in her throat. Dear God, what did he think he was doing? He circled the intruder, slowly, eventually putting himself between her and the threat.

No! her mind screamed. She started to reach for him but the other man's voice stopped her, "Don't move."

How could he see her…? He couldn't. He'd sensed her motion. Adam had done that once or twice, only his ability wasn't quite so keen. This man was far more dangerous than Adam. Defeat dragged at her, weighing her down until she felt capable of nothing but surrender.

It was over.

She couldn't win this battle.

She would never know exactly why her father had died or who had killed him. She would never know the real Adam.

ADAM STARED into fierce gray eyes, refusing to relent. He sensed a familiarity about this man, but he could not draw the knowledge to the surface. It was buried somewhere deep inside, a place he couldn't touch. A place that dribbled out information to him whenever it chose.

"Tell me your name," he commanded, his gaze never leaving his opponent's, the weapon pressed firmly against his chest. He didn't have to look to know that the barrel of the nine-millimeter had honed in on his chest as well.

"Cain."

The name reverberated through Adam, sent a kind of uncertainty washing over him.

"I've always been able to take you in hand-to-hand," Cain said. "This will be no exception. And if you kill me, they will only send someone else. Continue your resistance and you will be eliminated. There is no escape."

"And Dani?" Adam clenched his jaw, well aware of what was coming.

Cain shifted his gaze beyond Adam's shoulder, then back to him. "I'm here to protect her."

The statement stunned Adam. He'd expected the man to admit that he'd come to finish the failed mission. He'd expected anything but what he'd gotten.

He searched Cain's eyes, his face. "I don't believe you."

"Dani Archer," Cain called out. "Come to me, Dani. I'll take you to safety."

Adam sensed her easing closer. "No, Dani! He's lying."

She stilled.

"Adam is confused, Dani," Cain countered. Adam could see the lie in his eyes but his tone sounded genuine and urgent. "The injury he sustained before coming here has made him unstable. If you stay with him, you'll be in constant danger," he added persuasively. "Now, come to me and I'll get us out of here."

Dani stepped closer, too close. Adam urged her away, using all his mental strength, but she just kept coming. "Don't," he warned.

"How am I supposed to know if you're right?" she asked naively, standing right behind him. "What if he's telling the truth? If you resist, they'll eliminate you."

Don't let her believe him! The last thing he wanted was her trying to protect him. "He's lying about helping you!" Adam railed at her.

His attention shifted for one fraction of a second and Cain stole the advantage. In one smooth, fluid motion he twisted the rifle from Adam's hands before he could react.

"Step back," Cain ordered, his jaw hard, his gaze flinty.

Adam didn't move. To his horror, Dani did. She stepped forward, putting herself alongside him. She looked pale and terrified. Her body trembled as she sucked in an unsteady breath.

"I don't know what you or the people who sent you want from me," Dani told Cain with far more bravado than Adam would have preferred. He wanted her to stay back. She went on, "I don't know anything about my father's work. I only know he's dead. Haven't I suffered enough? Why don't you just leave me alone?"

Adam could feel her hysteria rising. Not good.

Cain shifted his full attention to her and in that marginal space in time, Adam acted, without hesitation this time. He pulled her behind him. "Stay there," he growled savagely. His heart rate picked up, sending a powerful surge of adrenaline through his veins. He'd been trained to remain calm under all conditions but he'd obviously forgotten how.

"I have very little time, Adam," Cain said, his tone impatient. "And even less patience. Stand down, *now*."

Adam backed up a step, forcing Dani to do the same. "The only way I'll stand down is if you follow your orders and eliminate me."

"Then you'll die." Cain leveled his aim at the center of Adam's chest.

Adam kept backing up, moving closer and closer to the rear exit of the house. Only a few more feet. He knew the door was open. He'd left it that way himself. The old-fashioned wooden screen door swung outward. She could lunge out that way. It was now or never.

"Run, Dani," he urged under his breath. "Cal and Rand are waiting at the end of the drive. They know what to do." They'd driven up to the house to feed the horses, Adam had intercepted them, sensing that trouble had already descended upon them. He'd taken one of their hunting rifles and instructed them to wait for Dani. They were to take her and drive as fast and as far away from here as possible.

"Move and he dies," Cain warned her. "Enough, Adam. It's over."

"Run, dammit," Adam roared, not daring to take his eyes off his opponent.

He saw Cain's finger tighten around the trigger and everything seemed to dissolve into slow motion. Adam felt Dani's hands suddenly land on his shoulder. She pushed with all her might, sending him staggering to one side.

He reached for her.

The gun blast exploded in the room.

Dani collapsed in his arms.

"No!" The word echoed on and on but changed nothing.

He dropped to his knees, cradling her in his arms. She stared at him for two beats and tried to speak before her eyes drifted shut. Adam's chest felt ready to implode, his eyes burned. Blood poured from the hole in her chest.

The still warm muzzle of Cain's weapon pressed against Adam's forehead. "Put her down and stand up."

Adam glared up at him, fury whipping through him

with such force that it was all he could do not to reach out and tear the bastard apart. "She'll die! I have to get her to a hospital."

"She's a traitor," Cain returned. "She's the one who sold out her father. That's why she had to be eliminated. You just don't remember. She is the *Judas.*"

"No," Adam bellowed. "They were wrong. She's innocent," he ground out. "She doesn't even know about Eugenics."

The Eugenics Project.

That was it. The Enforcers. He was an Enforcer. Cain was an Enforcer. The secret to the Eugenics Project had been at risk. Dr. Daniel Archer had been murdered in an attempt to steal it. His own daughter was thought to be the one who'd sold him out...but it wasn't true. She didn't know.

"She doesn't know," Adam muttered, his gut twisting in agony. "She doesn't know about any of it."

The pressure from the weapon's muzzle relaxed. "How can you be certain?"

Adam stared up at Cain in defeat, tears stinging his eyes as if he'd been hit with pepper spray. "She doesn't know. She never knew."

Cain looked at Dani, then back to Adam. He shrugged. "She's inconsequential. We have to go back. Put her down."

Though his memories remained muddled and his ability to think clearly and rationally still eluded him, Adam knew without question that nothing had ever hurt this badly.

Cain was the closest thing to a brother Adam had since both had been created and reared at Center. "Please, help me," he pleaded. "I can't let her die."

Adam remembered quite distinctly just then that Cain was different from him in one basic way. He possessed no human compassion. To appeal to him this way was like pleading with a rock. Pointless. He had to do something.

Pushing back to his feet, Dani in his arms, Adam snarled a warning, "Don't try to stop me." Cal and Rand were outside; they could drive them to a hospital. To hell with Cain. If he shot him, at least he and Dani would die together.

"Wait."

The solitary word, uttered with such intensity made Adam hesitate. "There's no time," he snapped, a part of him hoping the other man had changed his mind but knowing that the very idea was ludicrous.

Cain pulled out a cellular phone and pressed a single digit. "Send the chopper. We're ready to come in."

Adam frowned, not certain he liked the sound of that. Dani needed help now. The bleeding needed to be stopped. He didn't know what to do…felt helpless.

Cain stormed over to the sink and grabbed the dishtowel lying on the counter. He folded it and then pressed it over the wound in Dani's chest.

"We have to keep pressure on the wound to slow the bleeding." Cain took stock of the situation for a moment. "It's too low to have hit her heart or lungs." He bent down and looked at her back. When he raised up again his expression was grim. "No exit wound. That could be bad."

Before Adam could find the words to respond, he heard the sound of a helicopter. "We have to hurry," he said thinly. "We can't let her die."

Cain waved down the chopper. When they'd boarded, leaving Cal and Rand staring after them, faces worried, Cain pulled out his cell phone again.

The bleeding had slowed, but her respiration was too shallow and rapid. She felt too cool. Her eyes had not opened. Adam couldn't remember the training he'd had, but he did recognize that this was bad. Very bad. The pilot had estimated fifteen minutes to a large trauma center in Alexandria.

Fifteen minutes.

She could die in far less than fifteen minutes and there wasn't a damned thing he could do.

Cain put his phone away. "Center is sending someone from Medical."

Adam glanced at him uncertain what significance that statement carried.

Cain apparently recognized his questioning look and clarified, "Center staffs the most highly advanced medical team in the world."

"How long will it take?" Adam looked down at Dani's pale face. "It might be too late."

"The doctors at the hospital will do what they can. Stabilize her. When Medical arrives, they'll take over." He leveled a knowing gaze on Adam. "There are things they can do that others cannot."

Adam stared down at Dani and hoped Cain's words were true. The weaker she grew, the weaker he felt. He wasn't sure he could survive losing her; he was certain he didn't want to. Realization dawned on him then. For reasons he couldn't begin to understand, he knew with sudden and complete certainty that his survival depended solely on Dani.

It was all up to her now.

If she fought hard enough, was strong enough, they might just win.

ADAM SAT in a private waiting room, too physically and mentally exhausted to pace or even to think, for that matter. Director O'Riley sat nearby, no doubt waiting for the right moment to begin his interrogation again. Cain waited silently by the door.

Dani had been in surgery for three hours. The last report they'd gotten was that she was holding her own. The bullet had not damaged her lungs or heart. It had glanced off a rib, clipped her stomach and lodged in her appendix. The damage had taken time to repair, except the appendix, which had been removed quickly and easily.

Medical had arrived and were assisting. Adam had no idea what that meant since a team of surgeons were already in there, but Cain had said there were things they could do that no one else could.

Director O'Riley had interrogated Adam in depth already. He appeared satisfied that Dani had played no part in her father's betrayal and death.

More of the past had come back to Adam. There were still large chunks missing, but he had a fair accounting of his life. He'd been born and reared at Center. His education was extensive and extended to all elements of security and defense, including counterterrorism. His only family, of course, was eleven other Enforcers and the highly trained staff at Center.

"Let's talk about the letter again," O'Riley said, wading into Adam's disconcerting thoughts.

"I've told you all I know." Adam had remembered completing the first part of his mission, eliminating UN Secretary-General Donald Thurlo, a true traitor. He'd also recalled the letter. It was a very important piece of the puzzle. He had put it in his jacket, but he remembered nothing after that. Not the contents of the letter, not stopping to assist a stranded female motorist with a child in her arms.

"There are measures we can take," O'Riley began, "to attempt a retrieval."

Adam tensed. "What sort of measures?"

O'Riley nodded and Cain opened the door allowing another man to enter the small room.

"This is Lead Tech Fitzgerald. He'll explain the procedure," O'Riley told him.

Adam listened while the technician from Center's Research Department explained an optical memory scan. Recent memories were stored differently than long-term memories. In some cases, recent memories could be picked up in an optical scan. This technology belonged solely to Center. No one else on the planet had perfected the optical short-term memory scan.

"It's relatively painless," the tech went on. "And takes only a few minutes."

"They've set up a portable scanner in one of the rooms on this floor," O'Riley added. "Go with Fitzgerald. I'll let you know if we hear anything on Dani."

Adam started to argue, but saw the futility in the effort and followed the technician from the room. He might as well get this over with now. When Dani came out of surgery he planned to stay at her side.

"Is HE salvageable?" Cain asked.

O'Riley shrugged. "I'm not certain. His condition is weakening. That much is obvious. While they're doing the optical scan, Fitzgerald is going to do a couple other ones to determine the extent of the cerebral damage."

"And if he's no longer operational?" Cain persisted.

O'Riley couldn't decide if Cain cared or if he simply wanted to hear the grim details.

"Then he'll have to be eliminated from the program."

Something changed in Cain's eyes but O'Riley was damned if he could read it.

"What about the woman?"

O'Riley shrugged. "She knows more than is acceptable. I'll have to leave her fate up to the powers that be."

"She isn't a traitor," Cain reminded him.

O'Riley exhaled mightily. "That appears to be the case. But," he qualified, "she knows things now that could prove detrimental to our program."

"There may be another option," Cain offered.

"What kind of option?"

"One I think will work with the same accuracy and guarantee as elimination."

O'Riley lifted a skeptical brow. "Is that right? Well, don't keep me in suspense. Give."

"It's simple. She's in love with Adam. She will do anything to save him. As, I am sure, he will for her."

"You're certain of this analysis?"

Cain nodded. "Absolutely. She did take a bullet for him." He said this as dispassionately as if he'd remarked on the current weather.

O'Riley shrugged. "It could work."

"You'll have to test the subject, of course."

"Of course."

"And you'll reserve judgment on whether or not elimination is necessary until then."

"Until then," O'Riley agreed, surprised that Cain appeared to care one way or another. Maybe there was hope for him after all.

Chapter Fourteen

Adam sat at Dani's bedside watching her sleep. The urge to shed more tears was very nearly more than he could bear. She would recover fully. And she'd never have to worry about appendicitis, the surgeon had joked.

His eyes closed and Adam silently thanked God. He wasn't even sure he believed in God, but, just in case, he wanted to show his appreciation.

He touched Dani's hand, feeling the warmth. She'd felt so cold during that seemingly endless fifteen-minute flight to the hospital. The idea of losing her had shredded his insides somehow. He couldn't rationalize his feelings, couldn't pull himself together as he should.

Whatever was happening to him, he had no control over the situation. He felt less and less like an Enforcer with each passing hour. O'Riley had noted his weakening condition. The tech, Fitzgerald, had as well. The optical scan had not recovered the contents of the letter. Adam felt sure he would have read it before stashing it in his pocket, but he had no recall whatsoever of its contents. O'Riley intended to interrogate the two men who had ambushed him. He'd already had them questioned twice, but this time he would do it personally and he would ask specifically about the letter and the jacket.

Finding the letter might help them to locate Joseph Marsh and whomever he was working with. At this point, it was assumed that the Concern was behind the plot to steal Archer's files and ultimately the Eugenics Project. The two men who'd fooled Dani's faux uncle and who had attempted to kidnap her fit the profile of the type working for the Concern.

Adam didn't remember a lot about this group except that they were enemies of the United States and worked for profit rather than national security. Whatever they were up to, it wouldn't be good. As of yet, no one had been able to nail down the headquarters or its leader. The group was elusive and the members would gladly die rather than give up their peers or superiors.

All in all, it made for a no-win situation.

Joseph Marsh and the letter Donald Thurlo had possessed were the keys. It would take finding one or both to bring the Concern to its knees. The world would be a better place without it.

A light tap at the door drew Adam's attention there. He shook his head. Any other time, he would have sensed someone's approach. Damn, he was losing his touch completely.

When Adam opened the door, Doc stood in the corridor, a bountiful bouquet of flowers in hand. Adam glanced left, then right. Where was Cain? He had been pulling guard duty the last time Adam looked.

"How is she?" Doc asked, his face pained with worry.

"She's going to be okay," Adam told him, uneasy at the idea that the door was unattended.

"Can I come in?" Doc asked hopefully.

Adam nodded and stepped aside. He surveyed the corridor once more before going back into the room himself. This wasn't like Cain. Adam didn't understand.

Doc set the flowers on the table next to Dani's bed and moved to her side.

"She looks good." He nodded sagely. "They've an excellent staff here. She's in good hands."

Adam divided his attention between Dani and Doc. Something didn't feel right, but he couldn't quite put his finger on the problem. Maybe it was the idea that Cain had disappeared. He resisted the urge to sit down. What the hell was wrong with him? He felt utterly useless. Something was definitely wrong.

DANI HEARD voices. Adam. She smiled, or thought she did. She couldn't be sure. Wasn't sure where she was. Another voice. Doc. Oh, thank goodness. Doc was okay. He was here. Maybe he would help them.

An explosion echoed in her ears. An impact threw her against Adam.

She tensed as the memories tumbled one over the other through her mind. Cain. He was going to kill Adam. She had pushed him…out of the way.

The bullet had torn through her flesh, through muscles. Fire…pain. Adam looking at her, helpless, worried. Then nothing.

Where was she?

Dead?

Concentrating with all her might, she forced her eyes to open. Everything was blurry at first. She felt woozy, as if the room were spinning. She reached for her stomach but something stopped her.

An IV tube was attached to her right arm. She recognized the leads running from the monitor to her body, issuing a steady report on her vitals.

Hospital.

She was in a hospital.

"There's my girl."

She looked upward, her head swimming with the effort of refocusing. "Doc," she whispered. God, her throat hurt. Her mouth was so dry. "Water," she added rustily.

Adam was suddenly there, slipping between her and Doc. He moved a cup toward her, touched a straw to her lips. "You're going to be fine, Dani. Everything is all right now."

She frowned, wondering why Adam's expression didn't reflect his words.

The water felt good on her raw throat. Surgery. She'd been in surgery. That's why the raw throat. The intubation tube.

"What kind of damage?" she wanted to know.

Adam smiled this time. "Lost your appendix. Had to do a little repair work on your stomach. Fractured a rib. That's about it."

Didn't sound too bad. As long as he wasn't leaving anything out.

Another frown tugged at her brow. "Where's Cain? What happened?"

Adam took her hand in his. He still wore that silly T-shirt of her father's, Genius At Work. She couldn't help but smile in spite of everything. He looked so good. She wanted to have him hold her in his arms. To be sure everything was really all right.

"Cain saw things our way," Adam assured her. "He's the one who called for help. Everything is okay now. There's nothing else to worry about."

Again, that grim expression that belied his words.

She managed a negligible nod.

"I'm so sorry about those men," Doc said, moving in next to her again, forcing Adam to give him room.

She thought of her father. If he were here, they would have been doing the same thing. He and Doc had always fussed over her. Seeing Doc made her think of her father. She could smell the cherry pipe tobacco lingering on his tweed suit jacket. His white shirt was neatly pressed. Just like her father. Always looking the part of distinguished older gentleman. Tears welled in her eyes.

Doc's words plowed through her rambling thoughts. Men? "What?" Dani felt confused for a moment, then she remembered. Those horrible men who would have killed her had Adam not saved her. "No, Doc. That wasn't your fault. You didn't know."

He shook his head, staring down at where his hand lay against her arm. "I should have realized something was wrong. I shouldn't have trusted them."

She blinked back the tears that burned her eyes. "They said a colleague killed my father."

Doc looked startled. "What?"

Of course he would be. He still believed her father had died accidentally.

"I think it was Joseph Marsh who killed him, Doc," she said, losing her battle with the tears. One of the men who'd tried to kill her had said that her father's colleague had killed him, a man he had trusted. Marsh had pretended to warn him and all the while he'd been the one planning his murder. No way was it Adam. He'd cared too much for her father.

"I...I don't understand," Doc stuttered, looking baffled, and clearly unsettled.

"Dani," Adam said softly, "I'm not sure upsetting yourself like this is a good idea. You can give the details to Doc later."

"He has to know," Dani argued. "He could be in danger as well."

"Danger?" Doc parroted. "Dani, what's going on?"

She dreaded telling Doc this part. It would forever change his opinion of her father and that was the worst tragedy of all. Her gaze bumped into Adam's and she read his warning instantly. She shouldn't say too much. It wasn't safe.

It took a moment for her to determine how best to explain.

"Tell me what's going on," Doc urged.

"Father's work with the government involved certain projects that were highly classified and pertained to...to national security. Someone murdered him for information regarding those projects."

"That's unbelievable. I...I can't see anyone wanting to do your father harm," Doc stammered. "It's... unthinkable."

Dani knew just how he felt. "I know. I can't believe it myself. But it's true. A former colleague of my father's, Joseph Marsh, possibly, is the one behind the whole scheme. Whoever killed him needed a certain file." Victory warmed through her veins. By God, she'd thwarted that scheme. "But he'll never have the file now."

She felt Doc stiffen, his fingers clutched at her arm. "What do you mean?" he demanded.

Uneasy with his sudden change in tone, she tried to smile to lessen the building tension. He'd had a shock. Doc was only reacting as she had, with total disbelief and confusion. She suddenly felt exhausted. The painkillers and surgery had robbed her strength.

"Tell me, Dani," he pressed harshly. "What do you mean?"

"Doc, I don't under—"

He snatched his hand away from her and jerked a weapon from beneath his jacket. The air rushed from her lungs. What was he doing? Doc didn't carry a gun. Her father hadn't, either. They both hated guns.

"What did you mean when you said he would never have the file now?" Doc spat, his face turning beet-red with fury.

She shook her head. This couldn't—

"She burned it," Adam supplied for her. "There's nothing left to retrieve. It's gone." He said the last rather smugly.

Doc glowered at him. "I don't believe you!" He pointed that unholy gaze that bordered on madness back at Dani. "Tell me!"

"He's telling the truth," she said, forcing the words out around the emotion tightening her chest. Not Doc— he and her father had been like brothers.

"I burned the file and the tape of Marsh's call. That file cost my father his life," she said with a good deal more conviction. "I wanted to make sure it never hurt anyone else again."

"You fool!" Doc raved. "That file was worth millions!" He jabbed the gun closer to her. "They'll kill me if I don't hand it over."

Adam looked poised to make a move; she begged him with her eyes not to do anything rash. Foolishly, a part of her wanted to believe that Doc wouldn't have been involved unless his life depended upon it, but she knew better. "Why?" she asked faintly, her lips trembling. "Why would you let this happen? For the money?" She wanted to shake him. Tears flooded her eyes. This couldn't be…she tried to move, to reach for him, but the pain radiating through her body kept her still.

Something evil snapped in his eyes. "Why else? Of course for the money. Did you think I intended to spend the last years of my life in your father's shadow?" He laughed haughtily. "I think not. Opportunity knocked and I answered!"

She shook her head, confused. "How did you let things come to this?" Her head spun as a sudden burst of painkiller trickled into her veins. Not now! She needed to keep a clear head…to reason this out somehow…

"We grew up together," Doc snarled. "Went to school together. Only he got all the right offers, like that fellowship in genetics. I got nothing but what I worked for." He pounded on his chest with his free hand. "I never had anything given to me. I had to work for it!" He sneered hatefully. "While he went off to become a creative genius for the government, I had to eke out a living in a small-town practice that would never in a million years provide anything for retirement. Most men my age are on a golf course every day. But not me," he growled.

Dani felt too stunned or too drugged to respond. There had to be a way to stop this…to take it all back. This was too much.

"I was tired of him getting it all and me getting nothing," he snarled. "After he retired, I overhead a few of his conversations with Marsh. He tried to reason with your father, to get him to share his success with others, but the selfish bastard refused. I realized that was my chance."

"So you contacted Marsh," Adam spoke up. "The two of you devised a way for you to get the files."

"That's right," Doc said cruelly. "And I got everything except that damned code. The files are useless without it!" He looked at Dani with such sheer hatred that she shuddered at the force of it. "If you destroyed it—"

"She did," Adam broke in, his entire frame shimmering with an aura of danger. "Tell me, Doc, did you know when this started that you'd have to murder your life-long friend?"

Dani felt her heart jolt against her sternum. "No, Adam." She wouldn't believe that. Not Doc. Please, not Doc. The medication dragged at her consciousness, drawing her toward the restful darkness...not yet...she had to know...

Doc shrugged. "I made sure he didn't see it coming. It was all over in an instant."

"No!" Dani reached for him, pain searing through her. God, no!

Doc jammed the gun in her face. "Where's the code file?"

"Is everything all right in here?"

Doc jerked his head in the direction of a nurse stand-ing in the doorway. Adam lunged for the gun.

The blast thundered like an explosion in the quiet clinical setting.

The two men hit the floor. Adam quickly overpow-ered the older man and wrestled the gun out of his hand. A few seconds of heavy pressure in just the right spot and he lost consciousness.

Adam rocketed to his feet to ensure that Dani was safe and that the stray bullet had hit no one else. Fortu-nately, the slug had plowed into the metal bedside table on the opposite side of Dani's bed. Damn close. Adam exhaled a shaky breath.

"I'm okay," Dani assured him, the grogginess taking hold again as the adrenaline started to recede.

The pale-as-a-ghost nurse busily checked to see that her patient was indeed okay. Purposely keeping her gaze away from the men in the room, she fumbled with the IV tubing and leads connected to the monitor, then checked the bandage for seepage. Her hands shook as she went about her duties.

"Thank you for coming in when you did," Dani said to her while Adam secured Doc.

"Well," the nurse said, her voice quavering. "The way your heart rate was jumping around on the monitor, I had to come see what was going on." She heaved a big breath. "Never expected that."

Just then Cain breezed into the room.

Adam looked up, fury roaring through him. "Where the hell have you been?"

Cain smirked. "Right next door." He motioned toward the adjoining wall.

"What the hell were you doing over there?" Adam was on his feet now, staring down his smug colleague.

"This patient needs peace and quiet," the nurse warned. She patted Dani's arm. "I'll be at my station if you need anything else." She managed a tight smile before striding out of the room.

"You realize she will call security, who will likely call the police since there was gunfire," Cain said with bored amusement.

Adam jabbed him in the chest with his forefinger. "I don't give a damn who she calls. You should have been at your post."

"I was," he countered. "Had to make sure you could

still handle yourself. Maybe all is not lost after all. Besides, we had to see if Marsh or one of his cronies would take the bait."

Adam grabbed back control a mere second before he tore into Cain, which would likely end in his being hospitalized, considering his current condition. "You used her for bait?" Though the order would have come from O'Riley, Cain had obviously carried it out.

"You know the drill," was Cain's only response.

Adam forced himself to take slow, deep breaths. "Get him out of here before the cops arrive," he said instead of the litany of other things he wanted to say to Cain right now.

"Happy to oblige." He hefted the old man over one shoulder and tucked his weapon into his waistband. "I guess I'll be heading back to the Archer place."

"Why?"

This from Dani, who was frowning, first at one and then the other.

The idea that she could have been hurt again, that O'Riley had taken such a chance, sent a new rush of fury storming through Adam.

"Well," Cain said, turning his attention to her, "you didn't tell us you burned the file. You told us you didn't have it."

Adam started to make up an excuse for her, but Cain stopped him with an uplifted palm. "I'm not going to tell O'Riley. I just need to go back there and make sure there's nothing salvageable left. That okay with you two?"

"Fine," Adam said curtly. Damn, his head hurt and he was so tired. He felt confident that Cain wasn't actually asking for his permission.

"Thank you," Dani said, giving Cain pause when he would have headed for the door.

"I'm only doing my job," he said, determined not to connect with another human on that level.

"I know," she agreed, her voice thick from the painkiller in her IV. "I was thanking you for saving my life this morning despite the fact that you shot me."

Cain stared at her for a long moment before he walked out. Adam imagined that he hadn't known what to say. He was a hard-core assassin, the most violent Enforcer at Center; he wasn't accustomed to being thanked by his targets, especially one he'd shot.

Adam went to Dani's side, then he took her hand in his. "Are you sure you're all right?"

She looked sad, too sad. "I've lost my whole family. My father was murdered and Doc…well, he's dead to me as well." She closed her eyes for a long moment, then looked directly into his. "Please don't tell me I'm going to lose you, too."

He smiled and pressed a kiss to her forehead. "Not if I have anything to do with it." He kissed her cheek then. "Now go to sleep. You need some rest." He could already hear security running in the corridor. "I'll take care of this."

"I love you, you know," she said softly when she started for the door.

Adam looked back at her, too startled to speak. No

one had ever told him that. Something banded around his chest, and his throat suddenly felt closed. "Good," he croaked.

Then he walked out into the corridor to handle security.

As Dani drifted back to sleep, she had no idea that she would never see him again.

DANI WOKE slowly, felt groggy. Drugs, she decided. There was no pain, had to be drugs. She'd been shot. There would definitely be pain without drugs.

She licked her dry lips and forced her eyes fully open. The clock on the far wall showed quarter to twelve. She didn't know if it meant nearly noon or nearly midnight. How long had she been here?

Adam. Where was Adam? She wanted to tell him again how very much she loved him. She'd only admitted the truth to herself after...Doc. The emotion had been so strong and overwhelming she hadn't been able to keep it to herself.

Moving cautiously, she turned her face to the chair next to her bed.

Adam was not there; Director Richard O'Riley was.

He'd worked with her father...he was in charge of all this...or had she imagined that part?

"Hello, Dani," he said in that kind voice she recognized. He'd always been so nice to her. But was he part of this?

God, please don't let him be one of the bad guys as well. She'd had all the shootouts and brawls she could tolerate for one lifetime.

"Where's Adam?"

Director O'Riley stood, moved to her side. "There are a few things we have to talk about, Dani."

Adam. With utter clarity, she suddenly knew she wasn't going to see him again.

Her heart fractured.

"Your father was a great man," O'Riley began. "His death was a travesty to this nation and mankind in general. I want you to know that we will stop at nothing to bring down the people responsible for his murder."

Tears welled in her eyes and she nodded. "Thank you. That means a lot to me." She knew that meant Doc. God, how could Doc have done this?

"There are things, Dani, that you've heard during the course of this nightmare that are highly classified...that involve national security."

She swiped at her eyes with the hand that wasn't encumbered with IVs. "I understand. You don't have to worry, Mr. O'Riley, I don't ever want to think of any of it again. I also won't hold it against you for trying to have me killed. You thought you were avenging my father's death."

"That's what I want to hear, Dani." He patted her hand. "You realize that it's my job to see that the people who carry on your father's work are protected. That our great nation is protected. Sometimes I have to make tough decisions."

She nodded. "Yes. I know. I won't tell anyone." She bit back a sob, so afraid of what was coming. "What about Adam? Where is he?"

He patted her hand again, then tucked his own into his trouser pockets. "Adam's condition grew more and more unstable. I had to send him back to Center for treatment."

Fear stabbed into Dani's already damaged heart. "Is he going to be all right? Can I see him?"

"I believe there's hope, though I can't say for sure."

"I don't understand. He seemed fine." That wasn't true. She'd noticed him growing weaker. She was a doctor, for goodness sake. Why lie to herself?

"We're working under the assumption that he'll recover," was all that O'Riley would say on the matter.

"Will he return to his…to the work he used to do?" she ventured, not wanting to sound too curious but desperate to know what would become of him. She licked her lips again. Her mouth felt so dry. She was trying to be careful…to say all the right things to protect Adam as well as herself.

O'Riley studied her a moment, then said, "I'm not sure his recovery will extend to that degree. You can rest assured, however, that we will take very good care of him and that he will have a purpose in life."

It was all she could do not to cry outright. There were so many things she wanted to ask. So many clarifications she needed to understand fully. "I can't see him one last time?" she asked—pleaded, actually. She tried to keep her voice steady but failed miserably.

"I'm afraid not, Dani. It would be better if we ended things here and now."

"But I—"

"In fact," he said, cutting her off, "in order for me to ensure Adam's continued participation in the program, I'll need an assurance from you that you will never speak of him or your father's work again. You will never, under any circumstances, attempt to contact him. This never happened. Do you understand what I'm saying, Dani?"

Panic slid through her veins as if it had been introduced into her IV bag. She knew exactly what he meant. She'd learned the hard way over the past week or so. These people played for keeps. "If I don't agree to your terms, Adam will be removed from the program... and...and eliminated."

O'Riley nodded. "That's a fair assessment."

She swallowed at the emotion clogging her throat. "You have my word," she managed to blurt.

He patted her hand one last time. She closed her eyes and fought the need to shudder in revulsion. "Very good, Dani. I'll count on you." He smiled kindly, the smile he'd always given her in the past, as if nothing he'd just said had ever passed his lips. "You get well now, young lady. I'll be keeping an eye on you. Your father would have wanted me to look out for you."

Dani fought to hold back the tears until the bastard had left her room. She would not cry in front of him.

He paused at the door and she wanted to scream. "Goodbye, Dani. And remember, Adam is depending on you."

He walked away.

The sound of his footsteps carried in the long tiled corridor.

When they stopped, she could imagine him waiting for the elevator, content with himself. All was right again in his world.

But hers would never be right again.

"IT'S DONE?"

Cain waited near the elevator.

O'Riley stabbed the call button. He was tired. His frustration level had reached its limit. "You have to ask?"

Cain smirked. "I don't know why you didn't just send in Aidan in the first place. He could have read her recent past and told you she wasn't guilty, saving all of us the trouble."

O'Riley resisted the urge to say what was on his mind. "We didn't need his specialty on this one," he muttered, uncertain why he bothered. He'd had his reasons for choosing Adam. Aidan was a seer, not an assassin. The overwhelming evidence had indicated that Dani was guilty. There had been no reason to believe otherwise. They now recognized that Marsh had likely planted that evidence.

As they stepped into the elevator, Cain made a sound that was probably meant to be a laugh but came out more like a grunt. "Just as well. I have no tolerance for his constant mental roving."

That was Cain's primary problem, O'Riley mused. He had no tolerance for much of anything. But, like all Enforcers, he had assets no one else on Earth possessed. Each Enforcer was special in his own right. Unique... untouchable.

The elevator doors slid closed and O'Riley knew a moment's relief. At least now they had Daniel Archer's murderer and one of the players in this whole mess.

But somewhere out there was Joseph Marsh, a man who would sell out their secrets, giving those less than worthy the power of this ultimate group of genetically enhanced superhumans. Marsh had to be found. Those who'd hired him had to be stopped.

O'Riley couldn't relax his guard until he'd accomplished that goal.

No one at Center could.

Too much was at risk. *Everything* was at risk.

Chapter Fifteen

Three months later

Dani arched her back, stretching out the aching muscles. God she was tired. Twelve hours on ER duty would do that. Finally, it was time for her shift to end. She couldn't wait to get home and soak her feet. Heck, maybe she'd just soak her whole body.

She laughed at that as she tugged her sweater and purse from her locker. Such good intentions. She knew the routine. By the time she got home to her too quiet apartment, fed the fish, her new pet, and scarfed down a microwave dinner, she'd be asleep on the couch. It happened all the time now.

Her obstetrician had assured her it was all perfectly normal. The first trimester of a pregnancy was the most difficult to adjust to. Hormones were changing. Things were happening. She pressed her hand to her still flat tummy and smiled. But it would all be worth the trouble six months from now.

Center may have taken Adam away from her, but

they couldn't take the child she and Adam had created during that one night of lovemaking. She closed her eyes. Sometimes she could still feel him…if she concentrated really hard. That connection would almost come. Her eyes opened as sadness swept over her. It hurt too much…better not to open herself to the pain.

She drew in a deep, determined breath. If Center ever tried to take her child, she would run. She'd been saving just in case. She'd sold the ranch and the horses, stashed the proceeds into money market accounts and was allowing the interest to build. She had herself quite a nice little nest egg. If anyone tried to interfere with her life or her child's, she would take the money and run. She'd studied just how to disappear. Had taken additional self-defense lessons. She would never be caught helpless again.

Never.

She closed her locker and pushed away thoughts of Adam. She couldn't, not even after three months, think of him without crying. She would not spend her pregnancy in tears. She wanted this baby to be happy. That was her sole mission in life now.

Nurturing and loving Adam's child.

Nothing else mattered.

As she slipped on her sweater, the lounge door opened and Dani looked up, expecting to see one of the other doctors on duty or perhaps one of the harried nurses.

A man stepped inside the lounge and closed the door behind him.

Her mouth dropped open and her eyes widened in shock.

Adam.

Dani snapped her mouth shut and closed her eyes to the count of ten. Lord, she hoped delusions weren't one of the side effects of early pregnancy as well. She couldn't remember reading anything about them or hearing about any such problems during her obstetrics rotation. But then there was always the exception. Maybe thoughts of Adam had prompted her mind to conjure his image. That's all it could be. Foolish, wishful thinking.

She opened her eyes and he was still there...only closer now. Her breath caught. She pressed her hand to her chest and blinked at the emotion welling in her eyes. He looked so good. Jeans and a denim jacket. And underneath a T-shirt. Genius At Work. He'd kept the shirt. Her heart shuddered in her chest. It was him. It couldn't be anyone else.

"Hello, Dani."

She trembled at the sound of his voice. She would never, ever forget that voice. "It's really you," she said brokenly, then bit her lip to keep from embarrassing herself by crying. She'd fantasized about this moment... wished it could happen, but she'd known it was impossible. How could he be here now?

"Not exactly," he said mysteriously. He moved a step closer.

She frowned, worry sending a rush of hot, then cold, through her. Hormones. Her every emotion set off a conflicting flood. "What do you mean?"

"My name has changed. I have a new past and a new job."

Confused, she reached out to him, touched him just to be certain he was really there. "I don't understand."

"Center decided I couldn't be an Enforcer any longer. The injuries I sustained left me pretty much a normal guy."

She had to laugh at that. Adam would never be a normal guy. "So…" She cleared her throat. "So they just let you leave?"

O'Riley had said Adam would be eliminated. She stilled. Or had she been the one to say that? He'd certainly insinuated as much.

"My name is Sean Novak. I'm a detective with the San Diego robbery and homicide department. I just transferred in from Chicago." He extended his hand. "It's nice to meet you."

Dani threw her arms around him and hugged him tight, the tears making their appearance in spite of her best efforts. "I've missed you so much," she murmured.

"I've missed you." He kissed her cheek, then her lips. "Missed you more than you can know."

There were so many things she wanted to say…to ask, but his kiss deepened. His strong arms wrapped around her and pulled her against that awesome chest. Tender and sweet soon turned frantic and passionate.

He drew back, his breath ragged. Her heart raced so hard she could scarcely draw a breath.

"Does this mean…?" She wanted to ask if he'd come here for her. Or was he just dropping by to let her know he was okay?

"This means I love you, Dani. I can't live another day

without you. You're all I've thought about for three long months. Please tell me that you still love me."

She'd told him that before…and he'd remembered. "How could I ever stop?"

They held each other for a long while, too over-whelmed to speak, too thankful to question. Just holding him was enough. Inhaling his special scent, feeling his body against hers.

Eventually, he looked down at her and smiled. "I almost forgot. I have a message for you from O'Riley."

She tensed, uncertain whether she wanted to hear from O'Riley again. "Yes?"

"He said to tell you that you'd passed his test with flying colors and that this was the least he could do for the daughter of an old friend."

Shock quaked through her. "You mean he arranged all this?"

Adam nodded. "I don't think he could bring himself to see it end any other way."

O'Riley hadn't been able to order Adam's elimination. Maybe the guy had a heart after all.

Oh, Lord. She had to tell him about the baby. "Adam—"

"Sean," he reminded with a grin.

"Sean," she relented, "I have a message for you."

He kissed her nose. "That you're taking me home and making wild, passionate love to me?" he suggested wickedly. "I haven't forgotten anything you taught me."

"That, too," she teased, then turned serious. She had so many questions for him. Things she needed to know under the circumstances. But those could wait. They had the rest of their lives. "We failed to use protection that night and…well…I…" She let go a big breath. "I got pregnant."

For about half a minute, he looked confused. Confusion morphed into shock then a big grin that made her heart do somersaults stretched across his handsome face. "A baby? We're going to have a baby?"

She nodded and pressed his hand to her tummy. "In about six months."

His silly grin abruptly drooped. "We're behind schedule," he said grimly.

She laughed nervously. "What?"

He looked at her so solemnly she felt a little burst of hysteria. She couldn't bear any bad news right now. "I've been preparing for the transition into civilian life for six weeks," he explained. "I've studied social etiquettes and my research indicates that marriage should have come first. We have to get married. Right away."

Dani laughed with genuine amusement this time. She hooked her arm in his and started for the door. Wild, passionate lovemaking came next. "Let's go home. We have some catching up to do."

He hesitated at the door, his expression solemn again. "Is there a rule that says we have to be at home and in a bed?" he asked innocently. Too innocently.

"Absolutely not," she replied, setting him straight on the matter. She could think of lots of other places. The car, the table, the whirlpool tub, the bathroom…

"Good." He flipped the lock on the lounge door, took

her purse from her and tossed it aside. He kissed her mouth, her nose, her cheeks, each in turn as he backed her against the locked door. "Then why waste any more time?"

He lifted her against him and she moaned with pleasure. "Shift just changed," she got out between gasps for air. "We should be safe for thirty minutes or so."

"Hmmm." He skimmed his lips along her throat. "Just enough time for an appetizer before the main course."

She touched him, cupped his bulging sex. "I can't wait for dessert."

He nipped her earlobe. "I'll see that it's worth the wait."

"No more talking," she murmured between frantic kisses.

The metal-on-metal glide of a zipper being lowered and the push of cotton fabric up and over hips, followed by the ripping of silk bikini panties, punctuated the heavy breathing that filled the ensuing silence.

He entered her in one quick thrust, bonding their bodies as one, completing the connection that had been there from the moment they met.

Just before he followed her over that edge of pure pleasure, she somehow remembered to say a quick thanks for this special gift. Her life would never have been complete without this man.

Epilogue

O'Riley stared out the window in his office, his thoughts always going back to the same thing. Angela. And how much he missed her. Marriages that lasted twenty years weren't supposed to end when the children had gone off to college. That was supposed to be the beginning of their time together. But it hadn't been.

It had been the beginning of the end.

His intercom buzzed, drawing him back into the room…his office, his home actually. God knew, the apartment he'd opted to take in Boulder wasn't home. He rarely even went there anymore. He should just let it go and save himself the money. For what? he mused.

Before he could answer the depressing question, his intercom buzzed again. He pressed the speaker button so he wouldn't have to bother lifting the handset. "What is it?"

His secretary's ever-optimistic voice filled the air in the room, "Director O'Riley, Congressman Winslow is here to see you."

"Send him in." O'Riley stabbed the button to disconnect and puffed out a frustrated breath. He hated surprises. That the congressman would fly all the way from D.C. for an impromptu meeting spoke volumes about the subject matter.

Trouble.

Bullshit.

Or both.

He stood and faced the door just as it opened. "Congressman, what a pleasure." He skirted his desk and offered his hand.

Winslow shook his hand, his expression somber.

Perfect.

"You may not think it's such a pleasure when I've given you the news."

Trouble.

"Have a seat." Rather than going around behind his desk, he joined the congressman at his small conference table. "Would you like some coffee or mineral water?"

The congressman held up a hand to indicate he wanted to dispense with the pleasantries.

"What's on your mind?" O'Riley asked jovially. Hell, he was beginning to sound like his secretary.

"The president has decided to cut funding for Project Eugenics."

If he'd said the frigging sky was falling, O'Riley wouldn't have been more shocked. "What?" The current administration had been strong supporters of the program. That on the eve of an election year the president would suddenly withdraw support didn't make sense. "There must be some misunderstanding."

Winslow shook his head slowly from side to side. "No misunderstanding. He point-blank told me that the party was over. He intends to channel our funds into conventional projects like foreign aid."

O'Riley clenched his jaw to prevent the things he wanted to say. He knew how this game was played. Obviously, a new group had captured the president's favor, made him an offer he couldn't refuse and were bucking for more foreign aid funds in return. Power was the name of the game and someone had just outmaneuvered the Collective. O'Riley resisted the urge to shake his head. Who cared if social security went bankrupt or if national health care continued to be a fantasy? No one with the right kind of power really cared. End of story.

"Who has enough pull to yank the rug out from under our feet at this stage of the game?" he demanded, his fury gaining momentum.

Winslow shrugged. "Who knows? Furthermore, what difference does it make? It's too late to do a damned thing about it."

O'Riley smiled. Oh, the congressman just didn't know him well enough. "It's never too late, sir," he said politely. "We'll just have to make sure the right candidate wins."

Winslow looked taken aback. "Good God, man, do you know what you're proposing? The election is too close. The only other viable candidate is a woman, for God's sake!"

O'Riley nodded. "A woman that a good number of voters have been clamoring for. With a little nudge here and there, we could make it happen. I think our boy has miscalculated our reach." He would live to regret it, O'Riley didn't add.

"How can we be sure she would go along with our plans?" Winslow argued, flustered.

"You let me handle that. Everyone has their—"

"Don't say it!" the congressman cut him off. "If you're planning to try and finagle a deal with this woman, I don't want to know about it."

O'Riley laughed. "Don't worry, sir, I wouldn't waste our money that way. No, no. I was about to say that everyone has his or her skeletons. She'll have one or two, count on it. If she needs prodding, then we'll dig up some bones."

"Why can't we simply do that now?" Winslow argued. "Surely there's something."

O'Riley dismissed the suggestion. "Our esteemed president is already a player, gotten too cocky. He thinks we can't manipulate him anymore. He's lost his fear. She, however, is young, eager, has only spent one term in the senate. She'll be a pushover. And *he* will learn a very valuable lesson. Being in the game doesn't necessarily equate to *staying* in the game."

"You do love teaching your lessons." Winslow folded his hands on the table and heaved a defeated sigh. "Fine. I'll leave it in your capable hands then. When you have what we need, I'll proceed."

"Keep in mind," O'Riley pointed out, "that we may not need anything. She may willingly support our project."

"That's possible," Winslow allowed. He furrowed

his brow in thought, then asked, "How's the investigation going?"

He didn't have to explain. There was only one ongoing investigation. *The investigation.* "We haven't located Marsh and have had no luck retrieving the lost letter."

Winslow shook his head. "You know this could turn into a very bad situation. We can't risk another incident like that last one."

"I'm very well aware of that, sir."

"By the way, how is Miss Archer? Are we still certain she poses no risk?"

"Positive," O'Riley assured the nosy old fart. Why was it he never cared how things were being handled until the subject of money arose?

"And Adam?" he prodded. "His situation has been resolved?"

"He has been eliminated from the program."

Winslow shook his head. "Too bad. He was such a glorious success."

"Yeah, too bad," O'Riley agreed. The congressman didn't have to know that Adam, aka Sean Novak, was living the good life in San Diego with his lovely wife. Nor did he need to know about the child. That could become a very sticky situation. O'Riley intended to make sure that information stayed secret.

He might be a lot of things, but he wasn't entirely an ogre. The child deserved both its parents. And Adam deserved a real life.

As he blocked out the congressman's pointless rambling, O'Riley mentally shrugged. Who knew? Maybe he was getting soft in his old age. The way he saw it, he'd simply facilitated a happy ending for all concerned in the Archer case. Wasn't a thing wrong with happy endings. They just didn't come along very often.

He'd learned that the hard way.

He thought about the woman, Caroline Winters, running for president on the Republican ticket. She might just be about to learn that life didn't always provide a happy ending herself. From what he knew of her history, she'd been born with a silver spoon in her mouth and had never wanted for anything since. Giving her credit, she'd worked hard to get where she was. She wanted to be president. Maybe the old saying was true—be careful what you wish for; you might just get it.

As O'Riley saw it, there was just one last question—was the world ready for a female president?

* * * * *

Coming next month from Harlequin Intrigue
EXECUTIVE BODYGUARD
the second installment in
THE ENFORCERS
miniseries.

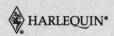

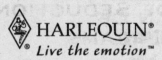

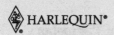

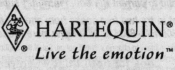

If you enjoyed what you just read,
then we've got an offer you can't resist!

Take 2 bestselling
love stories FREE!

Plus get a FREE surprise gift!